To love

The Stars We Never Saw

EMILIE GARRABRANT

ISBN: 979-8-9866757-0-1 paperback
ISBN: 979-8-9866757-2-5 e-book

CONTENTS

Café Herrenhof

August 1937, Vienna, Austria

The bright cluster of Cassiopeia stared up at the young girl from the faded pages of her book as she sipped a watery tea. The coffeehouse bustled with laughter and chatter. People crowded along the bar, spilling onto the outer terrace. The air was warm and sticky, and a small gust of cool air came through the terrace doors. The girl set down her book.

A slender, slightly older woman sat in front of the girl, deep in conversation with a man called Herr Adler. Herr Adler was the owner of the grocery on the street. He often took a mid-day break, usually in one of the nearby cafés so he could catch up with people rather than with the food they bought. Today, he chose Café Herrenhof.

Herr Adler was a soft-hearted, rotund man who waddled wherever he went. He had a black moustache that curled at the tips of his mouth and a genuine smile. He was always sweating and out of breath, as beads pooled at his forehead when he spoke. People loved him.

The elegant café is a nice break from our small flat, the girl thought to herself. She admired the botanical elements and antique chairs surrounding her spot in the cafe. Every seat was filled, with young writers scribbling ideas to elderly men lost in thought. The ornate gold detailing awed her every time she glanced up, as it seemed to look different every time. The owner had recently updated the decorations, and everything seemed homier now. This was the inner room, her favorite spot in the whole cafe.

"Herr, with all due respect, you cannot be serious in telling me that you haven't noticed heightened prejudice against us," the woman said. The young girl made a face, practically tasting the disdain in her voice.

The young girl cringed again. When the woman said "us", she meant the Jews of Vienna.

The young girl closed her book ever so slowly, so the woman wouldn't notice she was listening in.

Why is her banter about Jews all I hear? the young girl thought to herself.

The young girl couldn't hold it in. "Mother? What are you doing?" she questioned the woman. By now, her book was on the table.

"Hush, Ilse," Mother said tightly.

Ilse had eavesdropped on all her mother's conversations for months, picking up bits and pieces of what was going on in Europe, especially Austria. But she didn't really understand what her mother was saying.

A nasty German man named Hitler didn't like Jews. What did it matter? Vienna was in Austria, which was far, far away from Germany. Life was good here. Why couldn't her mother leave it alone?

"I just don't think this is going to go any further." Herr Adler spoke in a mellow tone, dabbing at a patch of sweat on his forehead.

"A majority of Austrians are supporting the anti-Jewish rhetoric and are calling for the Nazi promises to come to life," Mother continued.

Herr Adler bent down, shaking his head.

"Wiktoria, we can only hope for the best."

Mother leaned in to sip her lukewarm mélange, smiling slightly. Ilse could tell it wasn't even close to sincere, but Mother was trying to stay calm.

"Why don't you get back to the store? Trude must need you. Karl and I send our best," she said.

Karl. That was Ilse's father. Father was muscly and slim, and he had a small balding patch growing on the back of his head. Ilse often teased him about that. He had long bony fingers that played the piano with the ease of a swan. He always had a smile and playful energy that Ilse could never find from anyone else. Even after several hours at work, he would still greet her with enthusiasm, lifting her up into the air and tickling her until she couldn't breathe.

Father was the one who got Ilse interested in constellations, telling her stories of the stars, how they came to be, and anything she wanted to know about the universe beyond them. He read her stories, ranging from tales of Cepheus, the Ethiopian King, to fables of animals like Delphinus and Cygnus, the dolphin and swan. It was their special thing.

Ilse's mother had no intention of learning such stories. She considered it useless, as she did with many things.

Herr Adler heaved himself off the chair, a kind expression fixated on his face.

"So long!" he said, leaning on his cane. He bumbled out of the room.

Ilse shot an annoyed look at her mother. "Again? You have to scare off the entirety of Vienna with your foolish talk?" She fiddled with the corner of her page.

Mother shot a death stare at Ilse. "It is not appropriate for an eleven-year-old girl to listen in on adults' conversations."

"Mother, we're not even really Jewish. I don't even go to Hebrew school," Ilse complained. "Why must you always say these things—"

Mother narrowed her eyes at Ilse, lasering in her death stare. Ilse shut up.

Mother dressed particularly fancy today. The dressmaker had just imported the finest cloths from Italy, and Mother *had* to be the first to wear them, of course. She was wearing deep red lipstick, which made the dark brown mole at the corner of her lip pop. Her dress had a floral pattern, and the cut highlighted her slender body. Her gloves were on the table.

Everyone told Ilse she looked the spit of her mother.

They had the same sleek, fiery red hair that ended at their waists. Their eyes were the same hazel shade that could both captivate and scare you off at the same time. They had the same pointed chin. Mother's eyebrows were professionally trimmed, and she decided Ilse wasn't old enough to follow the same pattern. Ilse wasn't allowed to use makeup yet.

"We're leaving," Mother said. Ilse could see the whites of her eyes just sitting in front of her.

"You were talking right in front of me. Am I supposed to plug my ears? All I hear you talk about is whether somebody is going to come and take us away from our home. I'm tired of hearing this all of the time," Ilse groaned.

Mother sighed. "Ilse, it is not safe to be Jewish anymore. Your young mind can only live in a bubble for so long before you realize these things are out of your control."

Mother didn't sugarcoat things. If Ilse did something wrong, she would yell at Ilse. If Ilse did something good, she would congratulate her. Formally, of course. She did not baby Ilse like Ilse's friends' mothers did to them. And as much as Ilse appreciated her forwardness, she sometimes wished that Mother would let her be a child sometimes. Or at least more of one.

Mother glanced at the wall clock.

"Your father will be home soon," she said, raising her eyebrows playfully.

The corner of Ilse's lips began to raise.

"Let's go," Ilse said.

Mother put on her sunhat, slipped on her gloves, grabbed her purse, and then finally took Ilse's hand.

Ilse felt like a character in a movie as they made their way through the cafe. Some people turned to glance at them as they walked past. Ilse beamed, feeling even more beautiful alongside her mother.

"Dirty Jew," someone muttered.

Ilse whipped around, her hair blown across her face. What was that? Who said that?

Mother tugged at Ilse's arm urgently.

"Come along, Ilse." She spoke in a quiet, clear tone.

Ilse obeyed.

Mother dragged Ilse to the street outside of the cafe. Her nostrils flared and her cheeks reddened.

"Why did you acknowledge that insult? If you are provoked, you are to stay silent and not react, do you understand me? We cannot give them cause, Ilse." Mother made firm eye contact with Ilse.

Ilse's eyes widened and she bit her lip.

"Yes, Mother."

Mother upturned her nose proudly, acting as if she had accomplished something.

"Good. Let's go home," she said.

The apartment was on the corner of Zirkusgasse and Sperl, just two rights and a left from Am Hof Square. The building was painted a peachy color on the top two levels, and an off-white shade covered the bottom. The windows had arches at the top and were made of solid stone. There was a solid steel bar over the lower two windows, standard for the city. It completely contrasted the simple, white buildings that covered Vienna, but Ilse liked it. She felt that it made them special. Four families lived in the building.

Ilse's family had enough money to buy clothes, food, and mostly everything she wanted, but not enough for a large row house. Ilse didn't mind. She liked her apartment.

On the bottom floor to the left resided Old Lady Klara. She lived with her two cats. Ever since her husband died, she made nasty remarks about everything and everyone. She wore a black, drapey dress every single day. Ilse could never figure out if she had multiples of that particular dress, or if she wore the same one every day. She used to stare, to try and pick out any differences between the garments, but Mother caught her at it one too many times. Now, Ilse had to look out of the corner of her eye to spot any discrepancies. She always lingered in the hallway in her rocking chair, stroking her cats or commenting on the few passersby.

Across from Old Lady Klara lived a young German couple who had recently moved in. Nobody knew their names, or much about them. The young woman, a pretty blond, had recently given birth to a baby, and the man was always out of the apartment, presumably at work. Ilse saw them at the synagogue sometimes.

Past those two apartments was a windy staircase that took you to the second floor.

The staircase opened up in front of the residence of Frau Kofler, right above Old Lady Klara. She owned a sewing shop near the synagogue. The window of her shop opened up so that you could see her fixing your things at her desk. Frau Kofler had a large nose that was the perfect perch for her glasses as she squinted at the fabric and needle. Whenever she saw Ilse, she always gave a small smile or a nod, then continued on her work. She was quite mysterious to Ilse for no apparent reason. Out of all the people in the building, Ilse liked her best.

The Stadler family, Father, Mother and Ilse, lived in the last unit. Father had always wanted to be an astronomer, but his father pushed him to do something more "sensible." So, Father became a doctor. Thankfully, he still loves his job.

Mother came to Vienna from Warsaw when she was twelve years old to live with her brother, a university student, when her parents died. From there, she took up menial jobs here and there to make ends meet. Ilse felt that Mother could've been a model if she really wanted to.

"Married women with children don't model, Ilse," she would tell Ilse every time she brought it up. Ilse thought Mother was *so* old-fashioned.

The walls were thin, which meant everyone knew everyone's business.

Ilse knew Old Lady Klara struggled to move around, due to the crashes and clatters coming from behind her door. She also knew that the mother down below was stressed, unable to calm her crying baby and unable to hold down her household while her husband was out.

But Frau Kofler was a mystery. How could one be so quiet and collected in a building like theirs? It seemed that there was nothing wrong with her! Ilse didn't even know if she had a husband, children, or anything. *Maybe they were hiding inside*, Ilse thought.

Mother entered the building ahead of Ilse, strolling past Old Lady Klara. Ilse shuffled along, slightly scared of her after the fiasco at the coffeehouse.

Old Lady Klara rocked her chair slightly faster and let out a hoot. "What's a pretty girl like yourself doing cooped up in those fancy clothes? Let the girl play, Wiktoria," she said, taking a drag on her cigar. *I wish*, Ilse thought.

Mother pushed past Old Lady Klara without answering, and they climbed the stairs up to their floor. The stairs really weren't designed for more than one person at a time, so the whole thing squeaked and shuddered as the pair went clockwise and clockwise again.

Ilse dashed to the door, eager to see her father. She knocked, waiting for a response.

Moments later, the lock clicked and she saw his familiar, welcoming face.

Ilse squealed, jumping into his arms.

"How's my girl doing?" he said, carrying Ilse into the kitchen.

Mother followed and frowned. "Karl, I need to talk to you."

She looked at Ilse, her lips tightly pressed.

"Ilse, can you go to your room?" Mother asked.

Ilse pouted but obliged.

Father winked at Ilse. "You can tell me about your day later."

Ilse ran into her room, rolling herself into a ball on her small bed. She sat up and smiled when she realized that she could still listen into their conversation.

Ilse crept to her door and pressed her ear to it.

Ilse's room wasn't really meant to be a room. The apartment had one bedroom with a huge walk-in coat closet in the main hallway. The closet was big enough to hold a small mattress, so Ilse stayed here instead of in her parent's room. It was in a rather uncanny spot since the door faced the living room and kitchen instead of being near the entryway, where a closet should be. But that's what Ilse *loved*. Eccentricity.

Ilse's clothes were hung straight above her, and they tickled her face as she sat next to the door.

"Herr Adler is concerned about Germany. We weren't even in the district and somebody recognized us," Mother said quietly.

"The best thing we can do is act like nothing is wrong. We can't frighten Ilse," Father said.

Ilse beamed. She loved how her father thought of her. But why did Mother always say it was dangerous to be Jewish? What did that mean?

"What if Austria welcomes the Nazis with open arms? What then? How can we protect Ilse?" Mother whispered urgently.

Father sighed. "I didn't want to say anything until I had something confirmed. But since you're asking: I am working on a plan now. There isn't much of a resistance movement in Austria but I'm trying to find a place for Ilse to go in an emergency. It's not likely we'll use it, but just in case."

Ilse scrunched her nose. An emergency?

Why can't I just stay here? Ilse thought. She liked her room. She liked going to the synagogue, on the rare occasions they did. She liked reading in coffeeshops. Maybe she didn't like Old Lady Klara, but she liked knowing that she was always there.

Ilse scrunched her forehead. *Why were Mother and Father talking about turning my life upside down? What could make them so scared that they'd think of sending me away?* Ilse thought long and hard.

2

Anschluss

March 1938, Vienna, Austria

"Today, March 11, 1938, Chancellor Kurt von Schuschnigg has resigned office and cancelled the plebiscite to determine nationwide stances on the issue of Austria's religious affiliations," Father read in a wavering tone. Ilse didn't know what half these words meant.

Father threw his newspaper onto the table and lifted his hands behind his head in angst.

"What are we to do?" He walked around the room, patches of sweat blotting across his chest.

Mother's hands were shaking, and her coffee sloshed over the rim onto her skirt. Her makeup did no justice to the whitening of her face and watery eyes.

"Did you discuss with Fra—" She paused and glanced at Ilse.

"I'll go," Ilse mumbled. Ilse huffed, stomping to her room and covering her ears.

Ilse's parents hadn't stopped talking about Hitler. She burrowed into her bed, covering her head with her pillow. She still didn't really understand what was going on.

Ever since the ordeal at the coffeehouse, Mother hadn't taken Ilse out as much. Except for school, she was confined to their small living room. But nothing interesting happened at school, so Ilse didn't worry too much.

The balcony showed Ilse a slice of the city, but not enough to keep her entertained. If she leaned extra far, she could spot Herr Adler's grocery store.

Ilse had stolen bits and pieces of Father's newspaper, trying to figure out why she had to be scared of Hitler.

She knew *some* things.

She knew people didn't like Jews.

She knew that her parents thought Vienna wasn't safe anymore.

She knew people in Austria supported Hitler.

And she also knew that her parents were devising their own little plan for where she was to go in the event of an emergency.

But Ilse tried not to think about that one too much. She quivered. Would she have to be separated from them?

To be honest, Ilse couldn't see how Jewish people were so much worse compared to Catholic people. Jewish people practiced in a synagogue, and Catholics practiced in a church. As far as Ilse was able to tell, they had the same houses, watched the same movies, and drank the same water.

Ilse's family wasn't even *really* Jewish. Her father's parents just wanted their family to be members of the synagogue. They didn't go, other than for special occasions. It didn't make any sense to Ilse how that mattered to Hitler.

Light taps came from the door. Ilse rolled over. "Come in," she grumbled.

"Ilse."

Ilse uncovered her ears and stared at the ceiling. Father lowered himself down, sitting at the edge of her bed.

"I'm scared." Ilse blurted out.

"My child, you cannot be scared. Was Hercules scared, fighting the lion that threatened his people?" Father gave her a knowing look.

Ilse giggled. Father had told her the story of Hercules and the Nemean Lion so many times.

A powerful lion, called the Nemean Lion, had skin unable to be broken by arrows. He ate people and animals from the village he lived nearby. Hercules, the hero of the village, used the root of an olive tree to beat the lion, but to no avail. In the end, he fought with his bare hands to defeat the lion.

Father was right. Ilse had to defend herself, no matter what.

"I'm not scared." Ilse said proudly.

He laughed. "Of course not. Now, I need you to know some things. You simply must know this in order to survive. These are very serious and you must approach these with great care."

Ilse nodded, her eyes widening. What could be so serious that Father *had* to tell her?

"Good. First thing, never let on you are Jewish. Nobody can know this. From now on, you are Roman Catholic. Do you understand what I'm saying?"

Ilse's heart pounded. "Yes," she said blankly.

"I have managed to obtain forged documents for you." Father's eyebrows were furrowed.

"Who's going to ask for those?" Ilse asked.

Father breathed in deeply. "Officers. Anti-Semitists. A number of people could. Since it is not safe to be Jewish, we need to make sure you have an alternate identity in case somebody tries to hurt you."

Ilse didn't bother asking anymore questions.

Father revealed a large orange envelope, the size of a pillow. He removed a crinkled, crème-colored piece of paper from the package.

"This is your birth certificate."

The paper looked old and had a musty smell.

But something didn't look right.

Ilse Kofler was printed in solid black ink on the line labeled *Name*.

Under religion it said *Katholisch*.

Kofler? What did this have to do with the woman next door? A lump rose in Ilse's throat.

"Father? Why doesn't it say Ilse Stadler? There's been a malfunction. Can you get new papers?" Ilse rambled.

Father placed his hand on Ilse's. "We don't need to obey the religious customs of Catholics, but please understand me when I say this is just in case official papers are needed for examination."

Ilse nodded firmly. This would just be temporary. This was for her safety.

"These were expensive, so please take care of them. Secondly, I need you to know we have an escape for you when they come." He didn't say it, but Ilse knew. She noticed how he didn't want to call the Nazis by their name.

"But why is Frau Kofler involved?" Ilse questioned. She began to scratch at her nails.

"We live in the section of the city with most Jews, so it is likely in any event we are to be targeted first.

"Frau Kofler is not a Jew. She has family, friends, and papers to prove this. She is sympathetic to us and she is willing to take you in. You will pose as her daughter. When they come, your name is Ilse Kofler. When they come, you are a young girl that attends the public school. When they come, you are Catholic. When they come, you are a girl that works in your mother's sewing shop. Do you understand me?"

Tears welled up in his eyes, and Ilse followed, bawling into his chest.

"I am so sorry, my love."

Later on that night, Ilse awoke to her parents hovering over her. Father whispered something indistinct to Mother, and she shook Ilse gently by the shoulders.

There was barely enough room in the closet for Ilse to sit up, and she wondered how they had managed to fit in.

"Ilse, get up," Mother said in her steady voice. "I need you to pack a bag with as many clothes as you can fit in. Bring only essentials."

Mother motioned for Father to move out, and she dragged in Ilse's schoolbag.

At this time, Ilse was only half awake. The small fear of the unknown that she had carefully convinced herself to forget was coming back.

Ilse heaved herself off the bed and started squeezing pants, shirts, socks, underwear, and dresses into the large backpack. *What would I need?* Ilse thought. *Where am I even going?* Ilse squeezed her constellation storybook and her astronomy textbook into the side pocket. They were essentials to Ilse.

Ilse joined her parents in the living room and shot them a questioning look. The clock on the wall read six o'clock.

"The Germans have annexed Austria," Father said in a hoarse whisper. "As soon as Herr Adler found out, he awoke half the block."

"Senior Nazi officials are in the city and German troops and planes have already landed. Quickly now, cross through the hallway and go into Frau Kofler's apartment as if nothing is wrong. You are just awakening for school. We are the neighbors across the hall you nod to in order to be polite. Do you understand me?"

Blood rushed to her face, and Ilse grabbed hold of both her parents, hugging them like she never had.

"Go, Ilse," Mother said, a small tear running down her face.

Ilse's heart ached as she backed towards the door. "Goodbye," she choked out.

Ilse quickly slid the chain lock out of place and closed the door quietly, shutting her parents behind her.

Ilse walked up to Frau Kofler's door, half expecting her to open the door in perfect timing.

It didn't happen. But Ilse didn't want to knock. What if somebody heard?

Ilse slowly turned the doorknob, and to her surprise, it was unlocked. She poked her head in, her eyes widening in surprise.

For some reason, she expected the room to be bare, with one table, one chair, one spoon and one fork. One of everything for one person. Because Ilse had only ever seen Frau Kofler living in this apartment. Frau Kofler seemed minimalistic from the outside, but it certainly wasn't the case here.

The living room had an open floor plan, with an intricate rug and abstract tapestries on the wall. The couches and chairs were a lemon color, and a wooden coffee-table stood in the center of them all. Lamps were at the corner of every couch, and the small tables around the room each had stacks of books on them. A small lion statue was on the coffee-table. It was a truly beautiful room.

But it was hard not the notice the Catholic icons situated around the room.

On the coffee-table, Ilse saw the Virgin Mary holding the baby Jesus, while next to the modern-style tapestry she saw a Nativity scene. The Archangel Gabriel was above the couch. Everything seemed to clash, but in a relaxing way.

The kitchen was just the same as Ilse's, fairly small, but homey and kind. She could see a sewing machine and piles of fabric on the countertop.

To the left side of the room was a coat rack and Ilse noticed she had wrap coats, trench coats, fur coats, and more. Below were her shoes. Ilse recognized almost every type of shoe she had, from Mary-Janes and stilettos to boots and clogs. She truly was her mother's daughter.

A little farther back was a hallway, where Ilse could make out two doors.

Ilse took a step in the house. *I am to act as if everything was normal,* Ilse thought. Did that mean she should unpack? She shrugged and took off her boots, organizing them amongst Frau Kofler's pile.

A rustle came from behind the first door, and Ilse's breath stopped. Was this a trap? She backed behind the rack.

None other than Frau Kofler emerged from the door, who looked disheveled and exhausted. She was wrapped in a baby pink bathrobe and wore matching slippers.

Frau Kofler took a few dainty steps towards Ilse when she saw her. "Ilse! What a pleasure to see you," she said, a small smile forming. Ilse could tell she was careful to be quiet.

This was nothing like what Frau Kofler normally was like, Ilse thought. She always kept small talk to a hush. Frau Kofler never spoke to her. Nevertheless, Ilse tried to match her energy.

"Thank you so much for taking me in for the time being," Ilse said, inching closer to her. She put an emphasis on the time being, since she didn't want Frau Kofler to think they would be together for long. As nice as the apartment was, Ilse's real life was just across the hall. Not here.

"Where should I leave my things?" Ilse asked.

Frau Kofler came over to put her arm around Ilse's shoulder.

"Leave them in my closet, and unpack it. If we were to be searched, we would want them to think you live here," she said matter-of-factly.

Great. Another thing to worry about. Ilse thought.

"Why would we be searched?" she questioned.

Maybe this wasn't a good idea after all. I should've stayed with my parents. Ilse, in her head, began to run through the list of everything that could possibly go wrong. *The tea kettle could explode, the walls could cave in…*

"If the Nazis begin deportations, we need to be able to prove you live here. There cannot be evidence you are being hidden." She flinched, like a shiver had run down her spine.

A panic rushed through Ilse's body. "We're being deported?" Ilse said, a little too loudly.

"Hush, child. That's the worst-case scenario. After the excitement of the annexation cools off, you might be able to see your parents. They are just across the hall," Frau Kofler said, calmly. "For now, make yourself comfortable. You will sleep on the other side of my bed, as I don't have other spots for you."

She started walking towards the bedroom, so Ilse followed.

The interior of the bedroom matched the aesthetic of the living room, only this time there was no modern art.

The bed frame looked old, like it had been in her family a long time. The comforter was a soft, off-white color with cornflower blue pillows.

Other than the bed, not much was in the room, just a rack of clothes and a door Ilse assumed went to a closet.

On her bedside table was a picture of a man. He was handsome, with black hair that seemed to fluff or be messy no matter where you looked. He was standing with a much-younger Frau Kofler. She couldn't have been more than twenty.

Her ballgown was breathtaking.

The gown was a light color, fitted perfectly around the upper half of her body, then at the knee it flowed out into a silky trail. It was beaded and sequined. She wore silky gloves, one hand next to the man.

Ilse immediately recognized the grand arches soaring above and behind them. They were at the Vienna State Opera.

"That's my husband."

Ilse turned around, realizing Frau Kofler was still in the room.

A haze started to form in her eyes, and Ilse recognized a sense longing and pain in Frau Kofler.

Ilse stepped back.

"Where is he now?" Ilse questioned. Her curiosity always got the better of her, even in the most sensitive of situations.

Frau Kofler sighed.

Ilse bit her lip. *Did I go too far?* She asked herself that question many, many times.

Frau Kofler sat on her bed, and Ilse slowly leaned against her dresser.

"He passed away." Frau Kofler said.

"I'm sorry to hear that," Ilse said. What else could she say? In all the preparation Father had given her, they didn't go over the proper response for *this*.

"I made a sacrifice for him, Ilse," Frau Kofler said solemnly.

What kind of sacrifice? Why would she bring it up to me? Ilse didn't know how to reply, but she felt horrible for Frau Kofler.

"Let me tell you a little bit more about myself. Would you like that?" she said softly.

Ilse nodded.

"I was born Roman Catholic, close to Salzburg. When I met my husband, he was a student in university. He was... Jewish. My family hated him, and they tried to separate us. So, we eloped. His family still lives in the Salzburg area. I moved here so that he would feel comfortable."

Frau Kofler took another glance at the photo and revealed a small smile.

"After we had been married for four months, he took up a new job, outside of the district. It was still in the city, but the commute seemed horrendous to me. He said we would make more money and we could save for a child. And so, for the next two months, he would walk through the city, swinging past cars and buses dashing through the city. We couldn't afford a car, so he had to run the whole way."

She paused, fiddling with her ring.

"And well, one day his luck simply ran out. I don't know exactly what happened, just that he tried to dash through a crowded intersection. A car hit him and kept on going. It's a wonder they escaped in the traffic. That day was probably the worst of my entire life. I couldn't afford the hospital bills, but what difference did it make? Nothing could keep him alive. He passed on later that day."

She ran her fingers through her hair.

"I miss him every day, I really do."

Ilse scratched her head. *But still, why exactly was she telling me this?* Ilse wondered.

Her eyes focused on Ilse.

"Your parents wanted to keep you close. It must seem strange given we've been neighbors, yet strangers for all these years. Sometimes, when I stay up quite later, I can hear your parents talking. They are petrified. The Nazis are beginning to take control. Vienna is changing." Frau Kofler sighed, staring down at her hands. Her glance darted back up. "But I want you to know that my apartment is a safe place for you right now. Do you understand?"

Is she trying to say that I might lose my parents the same way she lost her husband? Ilse wondered. She had nothing more to say.

"I understand."

Kristallnacht

November 1938, Vienna, Austria

On a cool, November night later that year, Ilse was back in her room organizing the little things she had. When the hysteria had died down, and Frau Kofler discovered no one was going to take her parents away, she let Ilse go over for visits a few times a day. She wasn't sure if they were being watched, or if someone was looking for Ilse, so she had to be quiet. Ilse tucked some old history texts behind her storybooks. She hoped that Father wouldn't make her study them.

Life was back to normal, minus a few things.

Ilse hadn't been to school since the annexation; Frau Kofler decided it was too risky. Father's personality had changed. Instead of being easygoing and playful, he became more composed and serious. He tried to make Ilse study math on the few occasions that she went over, but it was too confusing without a teacher. *Why doesn't he want to spend time with me?* Ilse wondered. *Why does he care more about textbooks and math problems?* Mother was no help either. Ilse stopped studying English and German, and she stuck with what she knew.

A few minutes later, Ilse was laying on the floor of the living room, smoothing her fingers over the cracks and scratches on the wood. Ilse then realized that she was probably the prime maker of these marks.

"Ilse, get off the floor," Mother said. She was in the kitchen, boiling a pot of water.

"I'm going to die," Ilse groaned. "I'm so *bored*. There's nowhere else to go." It was either the floor or her bed, and she'd been in her room enough already.

"You're going back to Frau Kofler's after dinner. You'll be fine," Mother said nonchalantly.

Ilse heard a jingle in the doorframe, and she flopped over just in time to see Father come in the door. Ilse slumped back on the floor. *Maybe he'll laugh if he sees me!*

Ilse heard him take his shoes off and throw them to the corner, and then she heard his footsteps trail to the door. Another lock clicked.

Ilse sat up and looked around. He was in the bedroom.

Father didn't read to Ilse anymore. He never hung around the living room to play games. He never played the fiddle or the piano for Ilse to sing to. Ilse often sat with her ear pressed against Frau Kofler's door, so that she could hear her beloved Father open the door and go home. It hurt that Ilse couldn't run into his arms and have him tell her that everything would be alright. He came home straight from work, not even stopping to talk to Mother, and went straight to sleep. Ilse went over in the early morning once, to join them for breakfast, and she saw him wake up with sunken eyes. Father grew thinner each time Ilse saw him.

Mother put on a brave face, but Ilse could tell a small part of her withered away each time she read the word *Nazi*, or when she saw a soldier in the street. Her eyes no longer had the same glow that Ilse was proud to inherit.

As for Ilse herself, she felt somewhat numb inside—like this annexation was gnawing away at a part of her. Maybe Hitler's effect on the people around Ilse changed her more than what he hated her for.

"Ilse," Father said. Ilse turned around, and Father was standing behind her.

"Father!" she said. Ilse jumped up and hugged him. He loosely put his arms around her and glanced at Mother.

"I heard some news. Two days ago, a Polish Jew in France killed a German diplomat, an associate of Hitler's, and we do not know what this means for us. Get whatever else you want to bring to stay with Frau Kofler." Tears watered in his eyes, and for the first time in a while Ilse saw more than an exhausted face. She saw fear.

"But I was going back to Frau Kofler's for the night anyways," Ilse replied.

"You may have to go a few days without seeing us," Father said solemnly. "So take anything you would like."

Ilse turned, diving back into her room. She was tired of wearing the same things at Frau Kofler's so she knew that she had to bring more clothes. She grabbed her schoolbag and packed a mix of everything left in the room. Ilse was getting good at packing her life into a backpack.

Ilse took down her lilac party outfit. *Would I need a dress?* Ilse thought to herself for a moment. She fumbled with it for a few seconds, then put it back on the hanger. *I can just come back to get it if I really need it,* Ilse thought. She figured that since it was winter, warm clothes would be more useful.

There was still room in the side pockets for some small things. Ilse put in another one of her astronomy books and an English storybook. *Something* had to keep her entertained. Studying English by herself, though hard, would be better than staring at the wall.

Ilse's peace was broken by screams coming from the street. She left the bag in the corner of the closet and went into the living room. Mother and Father were peeking through the window over the balcony.

Ilse simply couldn't believe her eyes.

Herr Adler was being beaten by a group of men. Uniformed men with clubs hit him over the face, while a small crowd of onlookers cheered them on.

Why wasn't he at the grocery? Ilse wondered.

The store's front window was smashed in, covering the entire sidewalk shards of glass.

The sign he placed advertising the deals and sales at the store was trampled under the feet of the mob. The sign that normally said meat was twenty percent off was completely illegible.

His own words had come back to mock him.

"I just don't think this is going to go any further."

Father spoke in the silence of the apartment. "I need to speak to the rabbi. I'll be back, I promise. Give me five minutes."

He looked at Ilse and Mother and dashed to the door.

"KARL! KARL!" Mother cried. It made no difference; he was already gone. The door swung back and forth.

Ilse's palms started to sweat so she rubbed them off on her shirt. *Father will definitely come back. Father didn't break his promises,* Ilse thought.

Ilse went back to look out the balcony. Herr Adler was laying on the sidewalk, and her heart pained. Ilse wanted nothing more than to help him, but what could she do? She was only twelve years old.

Ilse then remembered the lesson her father had taught her. She must fight for others, no matter the risks.

"Mother, can I go downstairs?" Ilse wanted to help Herr Adler. Maybe if she got him inside, she could bandage him up.

"Stay here and wait for Father to come back, alright? Don't leave." Mother paced the room and tried to smooth out her hair. Her eye makeup was smeared and faded.

Ilse groaned. She thought Ilse wanted to see Father, but all she wanted was to help Herr Adler. Ilse glanced out the window at him, stricken on the ground, and turned around. Apparently, now Mother was blind to those in need. Ilse felt ashamed and embarrassed.

Minutes later, thumps came from the stairs, and the door flew open.

Father was out of breath. Sweat patches stained his armpits, and he smelled faintly of smoke.

"The synagogue's been destroyed. Windows are broken and glass is strewn all over the streets. Scrolls were on the ground, and almost all of the pews were smashed. I saw someone light one on fire and I ran here as fast as I could. Herr Adler was being beaten by a gang of Nazis and their sympathizers. There was nothing I could do," he said in despair.

"The whole street. The block," he said, waving his arms to the door, "is completely gone. There's wood all over the sidewalks, and the stores of Jews are being looted."

Mother collapsed onto the sofa. Father rushed to her. "Wiktoria, stay strong for me." He cradled her head in his arms. "There is a group of Nazi officers on the street. I saw some on my way to the synagogue, and they are arresting people. Ilse, go to Frau Kofler's."

Ilse was frozen in the middle of the room. *How could I leave? What will my parents do without me?* Ilse thought.

Mother sat up and outstretched her arms to Ilse.

"I love you. We will always love and be with you, no matter w—"

She was cut off by a smash coming from the downstairs hallway. Ilse rushed to open the door. Mother's face turned white as a rumble thundered through the halls.

Frau Kofler's door flew open in perfect timing to the wails of the baby below Ilse's apartment. Frau Kofler's widened eyes met Ilse's. She tried to mouth something, but Ilse was confused. She couldn't quite make out what Frau Kofler was trying to say.

A stern, authoritative voice spoke beneath them, the guttural tones echoing up the old staircase.

"I am an officer with the Third Reich. Show me your identification."

Ilse's body froze, and she felt her arms begin to shake. A shiver rushed down her spine, and she visibly shuddered. *They are here to take us away,* Ilse thought.

Ilse didn't hear a man's voice, so she assumed the husband wasn't home yet. She heard the woman stuttering something while trying to hush her son.

Frau Kofler was motioning for Ilse to come over to her. Ilse motioned to her back, trying to make Frau Kofler understand she didn't bring anymore clothes. She waved Ilse off, making the same motions to her side. Her expression grew panicked.

Ilse gently placed one foot forward, but she could vaguely sense the floorboards would creak with every step she took. The weight of her toe was enough to make a loud creak from the old flooring. *What if the officers hear me trying to cross over? What if they arrest my family?* Ilse began to panic.

"Give me the baby," the officer below said coldly.

"*Nein, NEIN!*" pleaded the mother.

"See if the child is circumcised," the officer barked. A grunt followed this, and the mother went silent. With fear, Ilse supposed.

Then: "Arrest them, I will check across the hall."

A few clicks sounded across the floor, and Ilse heard more raps.

"What are you looking for?" Ilse heard a cranky Old Lady Klara call out.

"Come with me, woman." The officer said coldly.

Ilse didn't hear a retort, as she would've expected, and the thud of Old Lady Klara's cane sounded against the floor. Had Old Lady Klara given up? Why wasn't she arguing back?

Frau Kofler's eyes were wild with despair. Her arms were raised above her head, waving in every direction, and she appeared to mimic stomping the ground. But she stopped as soon as her foot came close to the floor. She pointed to Ilse.

Me? Ilse mouthed to her. Frau Kofler nodded fiercely, tapping her wrist.

Was she trying to tell me to jump up and down? To… throw a tantrum? Now? Ilse turned her head sideways and gave Frau Kofler a questioning look.

Now, Frau Kofler mouthed.

Ilse grimaced. *I hope I didn't misinterpret her signals.*

Ilse turned to her parents, giving them a final longing look.

Ilse jumped, landing on the wooden floor with a deafening bam which shook the floor. She howled, beating her fists on the wall. Ilse wasn't exactly sure what the purpose of this was, but scared out of her wits, she kept up the act.

"*NEIN, NEIN, NEIN!*" Ilse rolled on the floor, sobbing her eyes out and yelling. The tears were real, since Ilse was petrified of the men downstairs.

The two officers came racing up the stairs. Ilse rolled around and began to kick at the air.

The first officer was much taller than Father and wore a uniform covered in golden badges and emblems. He had a mustache shaped like a painter's brush, which in Ilse's opinion, made him look ridiculous.

The second one was shorter and blond. His uniform seemed quite new, so Ilse could tell he was a rookie. He was no more than twenty-two.

"Is there a problem here?" the tall one sneered. *Did he think he caught us in some act? I hope Frau Kofler has a good plan. I'm sure we'll be arrested next,* Ilse thought.

The short one scoffed. "What a foolish girl," he said. He looked to the tall one for approval.

Frau Kofler spoke up. "I am so sorry, Officers. My daughter is throwing a tantrum, and she didn't want to come inside. Come on, my love, come over here."

Ilse shuffled across the hall, staring at her feet. She glanced out of the corner of her eye at the officers.

The short one turned towards the stairs, ready to descend. He was stopped by the tall officer extending his arm to cover the walkway.

"Why's the redhead your daughter?"

Ilse froze in the middle of the hallway.

The short officer turned, a smirk on his face.

Frau Kofler kept a composed image. "She is my daughter. Again, I'm so sorry t—"

"You really expect me to believe that's your daughter when the woman across from you is a red-haired woman?"

Mother was trembling, but Frau Kofler looked confident. Father's face was barely visible in the background.

He scoffed, walking up closer. "Show me your identification."

Mother and Father were hovering at the door frame in complete silence.

In one swift movement, Frau Kofler reached her arm behind the door and grabbed a similar envelope to the one Ilse's fake identification was in.

She removed a birth certificate, displaying it clearly to the officer.

"As you can see here, my name is Therese Kofler, born on August 11, 1905 in Maria Alm, Austria. My religion is *Katholisch*." She handed it to the tall one, while he held it up close to his face and examined it carefully.

"Alright," he said. "What about your *daughter*?" He said the last word in a sarcastic tone and a sneer.

Frau Kofler removed another birth certificate.

"Ilse Kofler, born April 19, 1926 in Vienna, Austria. Mother is Therese Kofler, Father is Oskar

Kofler. I am not Jewish, but I have a business in the area. The rent is more affordable for me."

She looked up to the man, her lips tightened. "What else will you be needing?"

The officer looked embarrassed. "I'm so sorry for the confusion, miss. I'll leave you on your way," he said, turning to Ilse's parents.

"Come my girl, let's have some tea?" She gently touched Ilse's shoulders, attempting to comfort her.

The pair slipped behind the door.

Frau Kofler raised her pointer finger to her lips and crouched down to press her ear to the door. Ilse followed her example, scared of what the man would do to her parents.

"Can I see your identification?" The older officer asked them.

Ilse heard some fumbling. A grunt from the officer stopped the rustling.

"You and your husband are Jewish?"

"Yes, but—"

"Move downstairs and await further notice. You are not to take any belongings with you."

Ilse heard Mother let out a sob, and she heard their footsteps slowly disappear into the night.

Ilse couldn't sleep that night.

Why didn't my parents have fake identification to match mine? Why couldn't we all be related to Frau Kofler? Ilse thought to herself. She thought about the envelope Father had kept her fake papers in. It was very thick.

Was it all for me?

Ilse's stomach lurched when she remembered what he said.

"These were expensive, so please take care of them."

That was when she realized her parents only bought her papers because they couldn't afford it for all of them.

The next morning, Ilse woke up feeling depleted. The screams hadn't stopped in the night. Neither had the cheers, breaking glass, or shrieks.

The questions didn't stop either.

Ilse wondered where the men took her parents.

Mother wouldn't be able to live in a crowded or dirty area for too long, so they probably moved her to a hotel. That had to be it. She liked the tearoom in the Waldorf Astoria on Fürichgasse best.

Ilse figured that Father would be okay boxed in with some other men. *Maybe he can tell them stories and teach them how to be a doctor,* she reassured herself. She rolled over in the bed.

The sheets were so soft and large, Ilse felt like she was drowning in them, and the pillows felt like feathers in a bundle.

Frau Kofler was still asleep, and Ilse could tell she would stay like that for a little while longer.

Ilse slipped out of the bedroom and tiptoed to the living room. The furniture stayed exactly the same, which gave her a slight feeling of stability. At least Frau Kofler hadn't changed, right?

Ilse sat down on the couch and took in the Catholic icons. She didn't know much about them, but now that she was supposed to be Catholic, Ilse figured she should learn about them.

"Good morning," a voice said behind Ilse.

Ilse turned around to see Frau Kofler walking slowly out of the room, wrapped in her pink robe. She had the same dark circles around her eyes Father had.

She smiled, which brightened Ilse's mood a little.

She made her way to the chair across from Ilse and sat down, crossing her legs. They sat in silence for some moments. Ilse stared at the ground, a multitude of questions circulating in her head. *Where are my parents?*

"I am here for you," she said. Ilse glanced up at the wall, biting her lip. "I am so sorry. I hope you will see your parents again."

Ilse looked to the side, locking eyes with Frau Kofler. She smiled. *I'm glad I'm not alone.*

The Bench

April 1932, Vienna, Austria

When Ilse was seven years old, Father would frequently take her to the Sigmund-Freud Park across from the Hotel Regina. It was only a few blocks away from the apartment. Typically, Mother would head to the tearoom in the hotel while Father and Ilse played.

The Sigmund-Freud Park was a large, flat area of grass that families often picnicked and laid blankets on. Father would prepare a basket with a red plaid blanket and sandwiches that he could snack on while Ilse ran around. Whenever it got extremely hot, large sprinklers would spray mist all over the park to cool the air down.

On one particular Saturday in April, the air conditioning in the apartment broke, and Ilse was soaked in sweat.

"*Mother*," Ilse groaned. "It's so hot. I can't *breathe*." Ilse was upside down, her head hanging off the couch and her feet up in the air.

"Ilse, sit straight up. It isn't proper for you sit like that," Mother said, reading a magazine. She didn't seem to be phased by the heat. And she was *completely* covered in a dress! Ilse was in play shorts and a thin shirt.

"Wiktoria, I think I'd better take her to the park," Father said. "It would be nice to get Ilse out. You of course, don't have to come. I know you don't like the outdoors too much."

Mother gave him a sideways glance before looking back at her magazine. "I'm not in any particular mood to go out. You two can go," she said.

Ilse glanced at Father, smiling.

Father prepared a picnic basket. When they were on the way down the stairs, Father whispered to Ilse, "I have a surprise for Mother."

Ilse was slightly ahead of Father. She turned around. "Really?" Ilse asked loudly.

"Hush, hush, we don't want her to hear," he said. "I'll tell you more when we get outside.

Old Lady Klara was in the apartment. Ilse could hear the crash and clatter of pots from behind the door. She dashed outside to avoid a confrontation.

"Tell me, tell me Father!" Ilse cried out. She was extremely curious. What surprise did he have for Mother?

Father held out his arm, and Ilse latched her arm around his. They walked down the street.

"Well, at the park, you must know there are many benches," Father said.

Ilse nodded. On the sidewalks, under the trees there were cute brown benches to leave your things on. Beautiful dedication plaques were nailed onto the center, and *so* many different kinds of people frequented them every day. One day, it could be a young art student, and another day it could be an old couple and their grandchildren.

"I spoke the park upkeep the other day," he said. "And they are putting in a new bench over one that snapped in half."

Ilse bowed her head solemnly. Antonia Nalder, a mischievous girl from her school, had jumped up and down on it and broke the bench. The bench had a special dedication plaque to the namesake of the park, Sigmund Freud.

"I am going to be sponsoring a new bench to be put into place over the old one," Father said. "And I'm going to write a very special message dedicated to your mother. I thought it could be a gift from both of us for her birthday."

Father was so thoughtful. *Imagine having a bench being dedicated to you!* Ilse thought. Mother's birthday was in May, which was only weeks away.

Ilse squealed, jumping up and down.

"What will we write on it?" Ilse asked.

The park was straight ahead of them. Lots of families frequented the center, and Ilse could see children running around. She beamed.

Father looked thoughtful. "I'm not sure, Ilse. We'll think about it when we meet the man who engraves it. He's just across the street, where the old bench used to sit."

The light turned red, and they crossed the street.

As soon as they made it across, a short man in a full work suit came up to them. He had a tooth missing in the front, and but his grin made him look *very* full of energy.

"Karl!" the man exclaimed.

Father reached out and shook his hand. "Herr Wieser, meet my daughter, Ilse," he said.

The man looked at Ilse with a huge smile on his face. "Nice to meet you! Let me show you to the plaque," he said.

Herr Wieser walked them over to a brand-new bench, but there wasn't a carved plaque on it. An untouched one was on the ground, smooth and shiny.

"I've got the plaque, I just need to know what to engrave it with," he said.

Father looked to Ilse, deep in thought. Ilse noticed that his left eyebrow went higher than his right when he was thinking.

Ilse was also thinking quite hard. She wanted something to symbolize the whole family, but she didn't want their *entire* name on the bench. It would be much too long. Just something special that only they could notice.

"Father, why don't we put all of our initials on the top?" Ilse asked.

Father looked happy at the thought. "Perfect idea! And let's put the message, 'We will always love each other.' What do you think?"

"I love it, and I think Mother might too. Our initials can go at the top," Ilse said, squatting on the sidewalk. The sun would've been right in my face if she had stood.

Father pulled out a piece of paper and a pencil. He wrote something down and handed it to Herr Wieser. Herr Wieser cracked his neck to the side, then knelt down with his carving tools.

"Time for the hard work," he said.

Father and Ilse watched his machine make noise and spin about, little chips of the plaque flying in all directions. The heat continued to blaze down on them, and Father kept wiping his face with his shirt. Ilse regretted not bringing water.

"Herr, you almost done yet?" Father said impatiently. They had been standing for who *knows* how long.

"I've just finished the initials. Come back and find me later, it'll be a while more." Herr Wieser said. His hands looked thin and trembly, and Ilse didn't dare to see how the letters came out.

Just then, a blast from a sprinkler came from right in front of Father, and Ilse jumped and yelled as it soaked him right in the face.

"Father," Ilse called out. "You're covered in water!" She was laughing uncontrollably by now.

Father's mouth was still wide open, and he was clearly still in shock. He wiped the water out of his eyes.

"On the bright side, at least I'm not so hot anymore," he said playfully.

Ilse laughed so loud that people were starting to look at them, but she didn't care.

Ilse turned around and spotted a gelato shop across the street. She tugged at Father's hand, pointing. "Maybe you can dry off here," she said.

"Ah perfect, Ilse," he said. "Just what I needed."

They ran across the street when the light was still green, desperate for some cool air. Ilse noticed that Father's shirt was stained all over with damp patches of water.

When they entered the store, a thin old lady was standing behind the gelato display. She looked very uptight and her lips pursed when she looked at Father and Ilse, a heaping pile of sweat and hunger.

Ilse dashed up to the counter, slamming her hands against the cool window.

Out of a sudden, the woman looked confused. She walked to the window and peered outside. "Did it rain?" she said to herself.

Father handed Ilse some money. "I'll take the vanilla," he whispered.

"Excuse me, Frau? Can I get a chocolate swirl and vanilla gelato in a cone?" Ilse asked.

The woman nodded, and proceeded to scoop them from their tubs. Ilse peered into the various tubs. The chocolate swirl was the most popular by far. The key lime pie tub was nearly full, so it probably wasn't as popular.

The woman set the gelato down on the counter, and Ilse handed her the coins. Ilse took the gelatos, walking to Father who had found a table in the back of the shop.

They collapsed, licking their gelatos for a while. Father checked the clock on the wall a little while later.

"Do you think Herr Wieser is done with the plaque?" Father asked.

Ilse nodded. "It's been a while. How much did the plaque cost you?"

Father chuckled. "Secret. What matters is that it will be there forever," he said wistfully.

"Not if Antonia Nalder gets ahold of it," Ilse said without thinking.

Father looked confused, but laughed anyways. "Let's go see how far along he is! I think Mother will be pleased," he said. They stood up, getting ready to leave.

"I feel like she wouldn't care for it. I mean, we can't even get her to come to the park!" Ilse exclaimed.

Father smiled. "When we were younger, she loved to come down here and walk with me. She's a lot sterner and somewhat strict, but don't believe it! Mother wasn't like that a long, long time ago," Father said. Ilse noticed he was smiling a lot whenever he talked about her. *Would I ever find someone who made me feel like that?* Ilse wondered.

Father and Ilse crossed the sidewalk, and the heat didn't feel all too bad anymore.

Herr Wieser was pressing the plaque against the bench. He was hitting it with a hammer.

Ilse dashed up to him. "Is it done?" she said breathlessly.

Herr Wieser stepped back, his hands outstretched, presenting the bench. "All done, Karl," he said proudly.

Father came up right behind Ilse, and they bent over to look at the detailing.

Ilse was amazed. She thought the carvings would've come out shaky and messy, but turns out Herr Wieser's got a talent for using that machine of his.

The first set of initials were Father's, *KS*, all the way to the left. The "K" was a little bigger than the "S." Next, was Ilse's, *IS*. Ilse liked to think of it as her being the bond and glue between her parents. That's why she was in the middle. Finally, all the way to the right were Mother's, *WS*. Beneath all these letters were the words, "We will always love each other."

Ilse leapt around, hugging Father. "I love it so much!"

Father laughed. "Hope that your mother likes it more than you," he said. "Let's go on home, shall we?"

5

As Life Unspools

January 1939, Vienna, Austria

Ilse could only describe her life in one way right now– it was like watching a spool of thread slowly unwind. First, you drop the thread, and watch it unravel its way across the floor. Normally, she'd try to chase after it till she could wrap it all up again. This time? There was nothing she could do to stop it.

The Nazis were the thread, running around and taking over Austria, while Ilse was running behind, hoping to avoid all the messes they left behind.

Everything was gone. Everything *had* been gone for months now. The building was a void. The doors from the night of broken glass remained unlocked, but Ilse was too scared to take a peek into any of them.

Ever since that night, Frau Kofler had kept Ilse inside. "What if someone's watching?" she had told Ilse.

Ilse didn't object. She didn't want to be taken from her either. Ilse slowly became attached to the couch, and she took in the books Frau Kofler had stacked around the apartment.

Ilse woke up and dragged herself to the living room to see Frau Kofler off to the shop. Frau Kofler was already in the kitchen preparing tea. Obviously, she was already ready for the day. Frau Kofler was always ready to go and alert. Soon, she would leave, and Ilse would be stuck inside for the rest of the day with virtually nothing to do.

"Ilse?" Frau Kofler said as she walked over to Ilse. She brought two steaming mugs of tea with her, setting it down on the coffee table. There wasn't much food at Frau Kofler's, but Ilse was too scared to complain. After all, she took Ilse in. She saved her life.

"Frau?" Ilse wondered what she wanted to talk about this time.

"Ilse, I've decided that sitting around the apartment all day is no good for you. It's been two months. You need to live a normal life. Come with me to the shop today." Frau Kofler peered down at Ilse.

Everything was so *boring*. Ilse didn't expect having no contact with anyone to take this big of a hit on her. At the same time, Ilse was even more scared to back out into the world. What if someone spoke to her, and she forgot how to speak? Would they report her?

Ilse looked at her expression. Frau Kofler looked quite serious.

"Oh alright," Ilse replied. She heaved herself off the couch. "What do you want me to wear? I have no good clothes."

"Nothing is too unsuitable for a sewing shop," she replied, raising her eyebrows and smiling a little.

Ilse eyed her, glancing back and forth at her pajamas and Frau Kofler's clean fur coat.

"Well, I *suppose* you should wear something a little more formal. Come with me," she said.

Not long after, Ilse was dressed in black tights and a plaid skirt and blouse. It felt almost like Mother was dolling her up to go out.

Ilse's door was the first thing she saw after coming out of Frau Kofler's apartment. It looked so lonely and sad. Ilse was scared to think of what was left behind, or if there even was anything left behind.

For the first time in two months, Ilse walked down the twisty staircase. It seemed more fragile under her weight than before. *Had I gained weight already? I was barely eating more than I had to,* Ilse thought.

Frau Kofler was confident. She'd been maintaining her life since, and this was obviously routine for her.

The carpets looked clean. No sleet, water, dust or dirt were present. However, Ilse could see a faint indent in the carpet where Frau Kofler's ankle length boots trod every day. She continued past, pushing open the door.

Ilse followed closely, but turned the doorknob of the couples' place as she walked by to see if it was locked. The door slowly opened when she gave it a push. Ilse quickly pulled it shut, scared to see what was left behind.

The pair strode down Zirkusgasse. Her legs felt like jelly, since she Ilse hadn't walked that far in so long. The road was empty of *life*. Sure, there were people, but everything seemed so *off.* There were no chatty families or street performers to accompany the beautiful buildings that made Vienna what it was. Herr Adler's store had pieces of cardboard taped over where the windows used to be. Everything looked so *gray* and *dull*. Ilse could see loads of uncollected garbage that lined parts of the street.

They turned left, and from there it was the three-block walk to the synagogue. Frau Kofler's store was just opposite it.

Once they got up closer to the synagogue, Ilse could tell that it looked the same as always. The outside housed two big domes, peach colored, and the stone looked as strong as ever.

Frau Kofler paid no mind to Ilse's wandering eyes as she unlocked the door to her shop.

Of course, her family didn't frequent the synagogue, but Ilse remembered a bit of what it looked like from the early days. Tall, grand and regal. But she didn't want to see what happened inside. The way Father described it made her never want to go near it again.

When Ilse first walked in, she was greeted by the presence of dust, but the colors of the dresses, tuxedos and shirts to be mended distracted her from it. A trifold mirror was to the left, propped in the middle of the wall for the best lighting. Stretching across the entire window was Frau Kofler's sewing station. It was weird being behind the glass, since Ilse had only ever seen it in the fleeting moments that her family passed the store. Ilse turned. Racks of clothes to be mended lined the back of the shop.

Frau Kofler tapped her nails on the desk. Ilse came out of her daze.

"Ilse, this shirt here," she said, holding up a navy-blue top, "–has a tear in the shoulder's seam. Poor Annika ripped it trying to take it off," she said. *How did she remember whose things were whose?* Ilse wondered.

Frau Kofler must've seen the look on Ilse's face, and she answered her question. "Sorry, I meant Frau Ebner. I know everyone in this neighborhood, Ilse. I remember things quite well." And then she pulled up a second chair to the sewing station.

It's funny how she seemed to know everyone, but *Ilse*, her *neighbor*, barely knew anything about her. *Maybe all the grown-ups knew each other, and the little ones were clueless,* Ilse thought. *How did she find all these people to know? Maybe they came to her shop, and friendships spiked over a needle.*

"Mend the seams. After that, you are to sew on a patch onto Frieda's blazer. It's set for delivery today. You can bring it to her apartment later on tonight," she said matter-of-factly.

Ilse tilted her head and squinted. Who was Frieda?

Frau Kofler was sewing a ripped dress, but somehow, she still saw Ilse out of the corner of her eye. "Frau Weitner. You probably don't know her, but she lives about two blocks from our building," she said. "Come to think of it, it's possible she's seen you out and about. You'll have to tell me what you find when you go there."

Ilse shrugged in reply, picking up the needle.

But why wasn't Frau Kofler concerned that someone might recognize her? After all, all the people on the block knew Ilse's family was Jewish. Ilse realized it long after she started sewing.

Maybe all the people were gone.

After Ilse sewed half of Vienna's blouses, trousers and everything in between, Frau Kofler decided it was time to go deliver the clothes. She would take Fraulein Kaufmann's blouse, Herr Mayr's trousers and Frau Buchberger's dress down Sperl since she was headed that way to the bread store. The rest of the clothes she mended could stay in the shop for pickups later.

Ilse was assigned Frau Weitner's blazer, since of course, she had sewed it. Frau Kofler was impressed with Ilse's sewing even though she never really did it before. Ilse made all her stitches very neat and small. *Frau Weitner would be proud to have such a nice blaze,* Ilse thought proudly. She neatly folded it into a brown paper bag and sealed it in tape.

"All set, Ilse?" Frau Kofler called to Ilse.

"I'm ready!" Ilse said. Frau Kofler was all the way at the back of the store, perusing through the racks.

Frau Kofler emerged from the cloth jungle a few seconds after. "I'm all set. I'm just taking these three down," she said, holding up the three hangers.

Ilse bundled up in her coat and went outside. Frau Kofler followed, locking the shop.

It was dark out, but Ilse could see the lights of buses and cars coming towards their direction. Vagrants milled about as they walked down the street.

Unusually, Ilse could see the stars quite well. She didn't have any distractions for a few minutes, so she looked up into the sky. *Are Father and Mother seeing the very same star I'm seeing right now?* Ilse wondered. She started to trace the shapes in the sky with her eyes.

Beep! Honk! Ilse heard a loud siren that pulled her out of her trance.

They reached the apartment soon after.

"Ilse, meet me back inside in twenty minutes. I want to discuss something with you," Frau Kofler said.

That was odd. They didn't exchange much conversation at the shop, so why did Frau Kofler want to wait till now to talk? Ilse shrugged it off.

"Alright," Ilse replied. "Where exactly is Frau Weitner?"

"Just one block down," she said, pointing down the street. "The building with a 555 on the front. On the right. You won't miss it."

They parted ways.

Ilse walked for a few minutes, and saw the 555 glittering under a lamppost before long. This wasn't just an apartment building; this was a townhouse. *Frau Weitner must have a lot of money,* Ilse thought. There were three windows on the top story with beautiful gold detail, and the bottom story had one window with a fake flowerpot on the window. The window panes were dark green. Ilse could make out the detailing under the light of the lamp that hung by the doorway.

Ilse rapped at the door, and soon a middle-aged woman with long, brunette hair answered the door. Frau Weitner could not have been more than thirty years old, though she had lots of forehead wrinkles. Her eyes were naturally wide, like she had just seen a ghost. Frau Weitner wore a blazer with gold and black cross patterns, a knitted skirt, and black tights. Ilse's home clothes were the exact opposite of this.

"What can I do for you?" the woman said in an overly sweet voice.

"Frau Weitner, I am working in Frau Kofler's sewing shop. This is your blazer." Ilse said.

Ilse presented the bag with her blazer.

The woman squinted at Ilse as she bent down to take the bag.

"Haven't I seen you around before? Do you frequent Café Grienstadl?" Frau Weitner said.

Ilse couldn't believe she was asking her this. They *definitely* didn't run in the same circles. Honestly, Ilse expected to see a maid to answer the door for her. Café Grienstadl was all the way in the first district near Hofburg. Ilse had never been.

"No, Frau." Ilse replied briefly.

Out of a sudden, she snapped her fingers. Her eyes grew even wider than before.

"You look like my son's doctor! Karl Stadler's daughter?" Frau Weitner questioned. "His office is near the park."

"Sorry, I don't know who you're talking about. My name is Ilse Kofler," Ilse replied. A lump rose in her throat, and she tried to cough it away.

"Anyways, I must be going, Frau. It is much too cold out here. Have a good evening," Ilse said. She rushed down the street.

Talking about Father made Ilse remember the bench they had put together years ago.

I should head back to the apartment. Frau Kofler must be waiting, Ilse thought.

Ilse looked up and down the block. Nobody was here tonight. Ilse realized that nobody would know what she was doing.

She took her chance, sprinting down the road, crossing intersections and running through red lights. Eventually, Ilse saw the familiar patch of green straight ahead of her just minutes after she started running. Ilse dropped to her knees, panting. It was *not* easy to run bundled in a skirt and jacket.

Ilse walked to the edge of the park, and she saw the familiar yet distant letters glimmer against the light of the street lamp. Ilse slowly approached the bench.

It looked just same as it had when Ilse was seven years old.

Ilse glazed her eyes over the initials, and she touched *IS*. Ilse Stadler, not Ilse Kofler. She was the daughter of Karl and Wiktoria Stadler, not Frau Kofler.

Ilse traced the letters with her fingers. *We will always love each other.*

In that moment, she had to hold onto that.

Maybe someday, they would return to the bench and find Ilse there.

Ilse kissed her finger and touched it to the plaque. "I'll see you some other time," she whispered.

Ilse rushed back down the street.

When Ilse got back, Frau Kofler was already waiting inside.

Ilse crossed the hall and closed the door. Frau Kofler had boiled some water for tea and cut some bread. It really wasn't much, but her thoughtfulness gave Ilse some warmth.

"Thank you," Ilse said, while placing her backpack by the pile of shoes.

Frau Kofler seemed quite solemn. She was sitting, cross-legged, at the counter. Frau Kofler stared at the table as she spoke.

"Ilse," she said in a quavering voice, "–I've been thinking for a few months. I've been thinking all day. I decided it would be best for you to leave Vienna. Your father wanted me to take care of you, and this is the best way to do that."

What? Why would she send me away? Where to? I had been no trouble to her. I was good. I helped out at the shop. A multitude of thoughts rushed through Ilse's head.

"Really?" Ilse asked. "How far do I have to go?" Ilse tried to sound more enthusiastic than she actually was. She didn't want to burden Frau Kofler by her pain.

"I haven't thought out all the details. I am sending letters to my sister. Her name is Gisela, and she lives in a small town near Salzburg. I–" she cut off. "I- I- think you would be best there."

"What town?" Ilse questioned. She had many more questions than that. Who was Gisela? How old was she? Was she kind?

"This town is called Maria Alm," she said, now eyeing Ilse. "It is buried deep in the Alps. It would be safe for you, unlike here in Vienna, where troops and raids are rampant. You need to assume a *completely* new identity. Not just your name."

Ilse's hands went clammy. She rubbed them against her thighs.

"I'll brief you on the details," she said, sitting next to Ilse.

Ilse turned to her, chewing on her fingernails anxiously. *Details? How complex was this plan of hers?* Ilse thought.

"You must tell anyone who asks the same exact story. Your name is Ilse Kofler. You are Gisela Kofler's niece from Vienna. You came to live with her to escape the violence in the city. You are Roman Catholic."

She paused for a moment to sip her water.

"Maria Alm is where my sister and I were born. We were raised there. People will wonder what has become of me," Frau Kofler said.

"But why? You don't send letters back home?" Ilse asked.

"Before my parents passed, the neighbors only knew I left town for Vienna. My parents and I's estranged relationship was probably for the best, since the townsfolk will have no idea what I've been up to. Gisela's been doing good about keeping my whereabouts on the down low. They don't know about the children I have or don't have. It also helps I haven't visited since I left to be with Oskar. My husband."

Ilse loved how she talked about him in the present tense.

Frau Kofler leaned back, resting her head on her fist.

"There's a beautiful little church in the center of town, near the square. As far as I know, there's a pizzeria owned by an Italian couple, Lorenzo and Giulia. I'm not sure if they still live there, you'd have to ask Gisela. The bed-and-breakfast is run by Gisela, though don't worry, it's not where you'll be staying. You'll get a lot more room in our house. The bakery-cafe was founded by Herr Berndhartt,

I think you'd like him. You'll meet everyone on your own time, so there's no need to fret," she said.

Ilse noticed that talking about the town seemed to sooth her. Ilse almost felt as if she was there right now, and not in Vienna. *It must've been really hard to pack up everything and leave it behind,* Ilse thought. *But that's what I'm doing too. I have to do what she did.*

"I must also tell you something else," she continued.

Ilse nodded. "Anything."

"Gisela once had a son. He passed of pneumonia when he was seven years old, and he is buried in the graveyard of the Maria Alm church. Be sensitive if you ever end up approaching this topic, do you understand me?" She gave Ilse a stern look. Ilse remembered how she had muffed it when she first heard about Oskar. Clearly, Frau Kofler remembered, too.

Still, Ilse was happy that Gisela found room in her heart to take in another child.

Ilse swallowed a lump in her throat. "Yes, I will."

"I have yet to discuss with Gisela when to bring you. Postage is extremely slow, especially this time of the year, so we'll have to wait it out. It could be three, four or five months before we hear anything. But it *will* work. You will be safe." Frau Kofler said.

6

To Maria Alm

June 1939, Vienna, Austria

It was summertime by the time Frau Kofler received a reply from Gisela. Ilse and Frau Kofler had just eaten dinner, and Frau Kofler had gone to check her mailbox.

"Gisela replied," Frau Kofler called to Ilse as she opened the door. Ilse was reading a book in the living room, but the second she heard those words she dashed to the counter. Frau Kofler immediately tore open the envelope.

Frau Kofler muttered a few words to herself, nodding here and there. But she also seemed frazzled. *What is she reading? I want to see,* Ilse thought. She fiddled with her nails.

Frau Kofler glanced up. "When you arrive, you will look for my sister on the train platform. She is going to be wearing a yellow top with a large bow, and a dark-green plaid skirt. She'll be wrapped in a plaid winter scarf."

To Ilse, this sounded exactly like what her mother would do. She dressed overly fancy and was always conspicuous. Ilse figured she wouldn't have trouble spotting this woman. But she was still confused.

"Frau Kofler?"

"Yes, dear?" She looked quite disheveled, and her hair was out of place.

"Where exactly am I arriving? And when?"

She inhaled. "Gisela is expecting you early morning June 19th at the Salzburg Main Station."

Ilse glanced at the wall, where a calendar was pinned. That's when she realized the dilemma.

"Frau Kofler, it's June 18th."

They locked eyes.

"Go get packed. Take only the essentials. Gisela can provide the rest." Frau Kofler said. "I'll brief you on the rest while we prepare."

Ilse dashed into the bedroom and began to shove her things into a suitcase and backpack. She tore her shirts and her coat off the hangers and haphazardly folded them into the suitcase.

"The trip to Salzburg is quite a long one. I will give you my Catholicism book and Bible. Brief yourself on the very basics: the Ten Commandments, the Seven Sacraments, the story of the Virgin Mary. You need to convince the town of Maria Alm that you are who you say you are. Religion isn't going to be that important, but what Catholic girl wouldn't know these things?"

Frau Kofler dug around in her shelves and brought out a religious textbook and a copy of the Bible. *A little above my ability, but I'll give it a try,* Ilse thought.

"This starts with the basics, no need to worry. Read the Bible during your religion class, just learn from the textbook for now."

"What should I call her?" Ilse asked. She didn't need to specify who.

Frau Kofler leaned back slightly, finishing off her bread slice.

"Tante Gisela would do just fine, since she will be your aunt. At the train-stop, she is supposed to be your mother, and I expect you to call her as such. It makes more sense for you to be coming home to your mother than your aunt."

Her tone was much more serious now, like a mother prepping her daughter for a school presentation.

Frau Kofler went to her nightstand and grabbed the newspaper, frantically flipping through. She drew her finger across it until she stopped suddenly.

"The last train leaves at 11:55pm. This one doesn't go directly to Salzburg, though. It will arrive in Linz at about two a.m. You will switch onto the train going to Salzburg from there. In the letter, Tante Gisela says you both will take a small bus to Maria."

A man with a halo was feeding bread to a goat. He had a long robe on, with a rope belt. Doves flocked around him, landing on his shoulders and on his head. Bunnies, ducks, foxes, and donkeys grazed peacefully around him.

Catholicism for the Young Mind, read the title. It was in a beautiful script, and Ilse could tell it was fairly old. Some of the front had scratches and dust over the details.

Ilse opened to the first story. *Adam and Eve, the first man and woman.* An old paper smell came from every page she turned.

Ilse had heard of them before. She learned about them *somewhere.* Everything looked way easier than she expected.

Do I have to follow these rules they have? It didn't look all that hard. I wasn't planning on killing anyone or anything like that. This was just for show, Ilse thought.

Everything will be fine.

The air felt thick and had the essence of a traditional train station. You had the smell of booze, cluttered garbage, yet also expensive perfume. The rush of the last train of the night definitely increased the sweaty smell arising in the room.

Ilse walked past rows of sooty trains, with Frau Kofler right behind her. She looked concerned.

"Where's the train?" Ilse asked.

Ilse glanced around the vast, open space where the trains were huddled. Train-goers were pushing and shoving, dragging baggage of all sizes with them. She couldn't believe it. *Who would be out this late?* Ilse wondered. She heard whining from a small boy standing a couple feet away from them.

A woman's face dripped with tears and she clung onto the boy. He was no more than four.

A station master came over the loudspeaker. "Vienna to Brussels, leaving in two minutes. Last call."

The woman crouched down, tidying the little boy's shirt, wiping off debris, and tucking it into his pants.

He had nothing with him but a tiny backpack, and Ilse felt so overly packed. Here she was, with five of everything she could carry, and the little boy probably didn't even have more than one change of clothes. Ilse bit her lip.

The lady planted him with kisses, and the child giggled. She unzipped his backpack, then opened her purse, pulling out an envelope. She turned him around and pushed the letter inside.

"Vienna to Brussels, leaving momentarily."

She grabbed him and lifted him up. The windows of the train to Brussels were open, and she pushed him through the window and into another herd of children.

It was then that Ilse noticed groups of parents lined up along the platform, waving and smiling at the children in the train.

A man in a uniform was strolling down the platform, looking at things around the train. Ilse presumed he was a conductor.

He glanced at Ilse and Frau Kofler.

"The train is leaving now, you know," he said. "Get the girl on the train, it's one of the last of the night."

Ilse tried to smile politely. "I'm heading on the train to Linz, sir. Thank you anyways," she said, trying to avoid eye contact with him.

Ilse stood, Frau Kofler's cold hand on her shoulder while we waited for the call.

"Vienna to Linz, boarding now."

Ilse glanced up to see Frau Kofler was already looking at her.

"Go on, child," she said.

Ilse obeyed, walking to the gap between the cars where a metal staircase was about to be folded up. She turned around, and Frau Kofler was waving to her. "Thank you for everything," Ilse called as the train honked its horn.

Ilse rushed inside, finding a seat on the side where she could see Frau Kofler. But the train had already begun to power up. Ilse couldn't find her knowing, confident eyes in the crowd.

Ilse felt the train chugging and sighing, as it slowly departed from the station.

Soon, the train was in Linz.

Ilse heard clicking coming from the cars in the front. *Will a stationmaster be inspecting my ticket?* Ilse wondered. She had often seen in the films Father took her to at the cinema.

Ilse unzipped her bag and held her precious identification close. She hauled her backpack around her shoulders so he could get out as soon as possible.

Click, click.

The door opened, and that's when Ilse realized where the heel clicks had come from.

A Nazi stood, brazen in his shiny shoes and crisply ironed uniform. He was a dark blond, with a mustache shaped like a walrus's. The hat covered most of his hair, and gave him an additional inch of height. The coat he wore was coffee-colored and had three large buttons in the front. The red armband had a swastika embroidered upon it.

A shiver went down Ilse's spine. Her heart froze, and her fingers started to become covered in sweat. She wiped them off on her shirt so she wouldn't smudge her identification.

His eyes locked on Ilse out of a sudden, and goosebumps shot down her arm. *Of course* he would focus on the one child on the train.

Ilse heard a call come from outside. "Last train for Salzburg leaving momentarily!"

That was her ride out. *I have to make it,* Ilse thought.

The Nazi made a beeline towards her. "What's a pretty girl like you doing alone on the train?" He placed his hands behind his back.

Ilse felt like throwing up and shaking, but she knew she *had* to maintain herself.

Ilse pulled her birth certificate out, holding it up to him delicately. She kept herself composed on the outside, ready to put on a show.

"Good evening, Officer. I am going to get off at this stop. I am meeting my aunt, to get away from the violence in Vienna."

The officer grabbed the paper aggressively, and Ilse winced. There was now an indent on the paper around his finger. He narrowed his eyes, slowly scanning the document. He brought it closer to his face.

Ilse swallowed shakily. *What if he's suspicious of me?* Ilse bit her lip.

After a few seconds had passed, she had an idea. It wasn't a good one, but it *might* just get her out of this predicament she had unfortunately landed herself in. She had to do what had to be done.

"From the dirty Jews."

The officer looked up, clearly stunned that Ilse, a small girl, had said something that bold. He let out a horrendous cackle, patting Ilse's head. In that moment, Ilse had a sudden urge to rip out all the hair he touched, every single strand.

"Go on your way, child."

Ilse nodded, taking the certificate and sliding it into the orange packet.

"Thank you, Officer."

Ilse walked out, calmly. As she got to the metal door dividing the cars, Ilse heard him talk to his partner that had marched in.

"Don't think we've got any," he muttered. "Reroute the next train. I think we've got some coming our way."

Ilse's stomach lurched, and she hurled herself off the train. She wanted to get as far away from that evil man and his cronies as she could.

Ilse dashed into the ticket booth on the platform. "Do you have any trains to Salzburg?"

The lady at the station looked through a schedule on the wall. "You like to cut it close, eh? The train leaves in about two minutes. Tickets are 260 schillings a piece."

Ilse's eyes widened. She didn't have any money. Ilse crouched down, sifting through her bag to see if Frau Kofler had dropped any loose change inside. There was nothing. She forgot to give Ilse change for the next train.

Ilse retreated to the bench situated outside the window and slumped. Now, she was stuck. There was a clock next to the booth, so she leaned over to read it. 2:07. Ilse groaned. She was supposed to be in Salzburg in an hour and a half.

The faint whistle of a train blew from behind Ilse, and people were suddenly on the platform, awaiting arrival.

Ilse scanned the platform. A lady with three young boys surrounding her was busy with another baby in her arms. Ilse stood up. *I can stand behind them! If I could make us look like a family boarding, this will be no problem,* Ilse thought. There were no more than twenty people attempting to board, so there would be room for her on the train.

The black train was almost entirely invisible in the nighttime dark. Red outlines highlighted the ends and curves, but other than that it blended with the night. Ilse followed the woman and the children, filing into the line.

Soon, it was her turn. Ilse huddled close to the group. This was her chance to get to Salzburg!

Ilse stayed huddled next to the boys as the ticket master looked over their tickets.

"You're one ticket short, ma'am. You've only got five."

Ilse's eyes widened, and she bit her lip. *Was he actually counting off the tickets?* Ilse wondered. *Oh no.*

The woman looked confused. She took off her glasses and rubbed her eyes.

"I've got my four children and myself, that's five in total."

"I see. I thought the girl behind you was with your group. Enjoy the ride," he said as they climbed aboard.

He turned to Ilse. "Ticket please," he said.

"I don't have one. I'm out of money. Can you let me on for free? I have to get home."

"Sorry, miss. No can do. WE'RE SET!" He yelled the last part extra loud, and somebody leaned out of the front caboose, signaling a thumbs up. He climbed up the stairs and folded the steps.

Alone on the platform, Ilse stared into the sky. Now she was stuck.

Her eyes wandered for a moment. That was when she noticed an open window in the back car. The light was on, but she didn't see any heads. It was empty back there.

Ilse remembered the mother lifting her son into the train right before it took off. *What if I did the same?* Ilse wondered.

Ilse set her foot on the connecting rod of the wheels. She bounced her foot up and down. It was enough to support her weight.

The horn blew, and she heard a chugging noise start to build up. This was her last chance!

Ilse stretched her hand up, trying to see if the window was in a reasonable distance. She was able to fit her hand around the opening. It looked wide enough for her alone to squeeze through, but the window definitely couldn't fit her backpack in as well.

Ilse quickly pulled the backpack off and tossed it through the window. Holding onto the edge of the window, she set one foot on the wheel and pushed off, possibly a little too hard, and went tumbling into the car.

7

Tante Gisela

June 1939, Maria Alm, Austria

The air was warm and dewy. The countryside was more visible under the lights of the Salzburg Main Station. The hills seemed to roll and go on for days. But Ilse could only see what the train station's light illuminated, which wasn't much.

While Ilse was standing in the station, she realized that she had never left Vienna before.

What did the stars look like in the country? Ilse wondered. She'd have to wait a little to find out. In Vienna, you could never find a moment of silence or peace, since a horn was always blaring, or smoke was in the air. Ilse figured that the country would be different.

A clock above the ticket booth read 3:15. The platform was slowly filling up with people.

"Ilse!" A woman's voice came from next to her.

Ilse turned around, slowly.

A young woman, probably around thirty, had tapped her on the shoulder. She looked just like Frau Kofler, but her hair was lighter and her face was completely smooth, like a model. It appeared slightly oily in the station light. Much like a button, her nose was small and round. She wore the very clothes Frau Kofler said she would wear, and the pineapple-color of her yellow top made Ilse think of food, while the bow made her look sophisticated.

The woman leaned down to Ilse's ear. "Gisela," she whispered.

"Mother!" Ilse spoke loud enough not to be suspicious, but she didn't *really* want anyone to think Gisela was her actual mother. Ilse thought that she looked nice, but she wasn't as pretty as her *real* mother. Ilse hugged her around the waist.

Gisela laughed, wrapping her arms around Ilse's back. She was much taller than Ilse.

"Let's get on home, shall we?"

Ilse linked her arm around Gisela's, and they walked out of the station. It felt weird, since obviously Ilse had never met her before. If Frau Kofler trusted her, Ilse figured she would too. It's not like she had a choice, really.

Ilse and Gisela walked out of the station and went to a small, sheltered bus stop a few streets down from the station. Nobody was there.

Ilse saw Gisela trace her gloved hand along the list of times for bus rides. She stopped.

"Our bus should be here soon, Ilse." Gisela sat down on the dirty bus bench, which had Ilse surprised. She seemed like a woman who would despise dirty bus stops, like Mother. Especially with her nice outfit on.

"I guess we haven't introduced ourselves," Ilse said hesitantly. She wasn't sure what their relationship would be like. *Would we be like close sisters, or a strict parent-child association? Or would she just be a caretaker I spoke to every now and then?* Ilse wondered.

Gisela smiled. "As you know, I am Gisela, and I'm Ther— Frau Kofler's sister." Her voice was soothing to listen to.

"I'll be your foster mother while you live with me in Maria Alm. You're supposed to be my niece, so you can call me Tante Gisela. It would be the proper term."

Ilse smiled and nodded.

"The people in Maria Alm know I'm bringing a little girl home. They haven't seen Frau Kofler since she left to marry her husband—and no one knows Oskar was Jewish or what he looked like—so they have no reason to doubt who you are. But I have to warn you, news travels fast. Be careful of whatever you say."

Ilse let out some small "yeah" and "yes" replies to things Tante Gisela asked her, but she was really focused on Salzburg. The streets were similar to Vienna, but wider, cleaner and less crowded. It was everything she'd imagined.

A cute red bus pulled up to the stop, and the doors opened slowly. They made loud creaking noises. Ilse questioned the functionality of the bus as Tante Gisela went up the steps. The bus was completely empty.

Ilse boarded and they both headed to the seats in the very back. Ilse picked a seat right by the window, and Tante Gisela sat down next to her.

They sat in silence for around forty minutes. Ilse was thinking about her parents the entire time. She wondered what Mother was doing right now. *She's probably reapplying her makeup,* Ilse thought. *Father was probably reading.*

Ilse suddenly remembered the Nazi on the train said he was rerouting. Where did he reroute it to? *Maybe that's where my parents were,* Ilse thought.

"Tante Gisela, I have a question."

Tante Gisela seemed to be in her own daze, but when Ilse spoke, she snapped back into reality.

"Yes, anything," Tante Gisela replied.

"Why do Nazis search trains?" Ilse questioned.

She turned her head, looking shocked and confused. Almost as if she knew something Ilse didn't. Now, Ilse wanted to know what she knew.

"How do you know about that?"

Ilse told her the story of how she got on the train, how a Nazi questioned her, and how she managed to sneak on a train to Salzburg,

Tante Gisela took a deep breath in. "They search to capture people. More often than not, to go death camps."

Ilse's heart slowed as she felt tears rushing to her eyes. Her chest pounded and she could feel her heart rate quicken.

"Jewish people are starting to be deported to death camps. I'm so sorry, Ilse."

Ilse inhaled, trying to slow her breath. Tears were running down her neck, and she wiped it off with her shirt. "Thank you for telling me." She appreciated that Tante Gisela was just as honest as Mother.

Tante Gisela hugged Ilse suddenly, pulling away after a few seconds.

"As soon as we get back, get into your room and settle in. I'll give you your privacy, alright?"

Ilse nodded.

The bus slowed to a halt, and Ilse looked out the window. It was pitch black, and she couldn't make out much, other than covered bus stop, with a streetlamp illuminating the spot. The gravel road left dust flying in the air.

"Thank you," Ilse said to the driver, hurrying off the bus. She was tired. Not to mention hungry.

Tante Gisela followed Ilse, putting her arm around Ilse's shoulder. The bus drove into the distance, and slowly became a sliver.

The pair walked the dirt road to the entrance of the town. It was so beautiful, Ilse forgot all her worries and doubts for an instant.

Night lights were strung, building to building, forming an archway along the main road. A part of the building poked out like a half-hexagon and Ilse could tell it was a dining room for a restaurant. The building all around were traditionally styled with creme colors and red detailing. Petunias and begonias hung from all the windows they passed. *Why was it so colorful? Were all small towns like that?* Ilse wondered. She couldn't make out much of the other stores.

The church was the tallest thing in the entire area, other than the mountains. It was fully illuminated and seemed to dominate the square like a monster. Yet, it was so beautiful and elegant. Ilse had never been in a Catholic church before, but she'd seen plenty in Vienna.

The tops of all the houses were just the same. A very wide, upside down "V" was the shape, with metal roofing. Wreaths of flowers were hung across decks and balconies. Everything was made of wood, of course. This was what Ilse had dreamed the Austrian countryside would look like.

Tante Gisela and Ilse walked in silence, rounding the church, and going to the houses behind it. Tante Gisela walked past a row of houses, then up a sloping side street. They turned the bend, going upwards.

There was only one house up ahead. It was identical to every other house in the town, but Ilse liked the privacy it had.

Tante Gisela stood, smiling. "Here it is. What do you think?"

Ilse gazed up in awe. The house was the size of her entire apartment building. "I love it so much," she said breathlessly.

They went up to the left side of the house, where Tante Gisela unlocked the door.

"Normally, I leave this door unlocked," she said. "You can use it whenever you need it."

Ilse could see they had a hill behind the house, and she saw a patch of trees at the top.

Ilse had an urge to go up there. She didn't know what pulled her, but she couldn't resist.

"Can I go up on the hill? I want to see what the town looks like," Ilse said. Well, that was only part of the reason.

Tante Gisela tilted her head. "I suppose. Be back down in ten minutes!" She began to take things out of her backpack, refolding and organizing them.

Ilse dashed out, closing the door with a slam. She dashed up the hill, running farther back on that flat area of the land. The town was breathtaking, with dots of light from porch lamps shining here and there. The church was so grand and regal amongst the backdrop of the mountains. But that wasn't even all. Ilse looked up, trying to catch her breath.

When Ilse saw the stars, she staggered backwards.

You can't see the sky in Vienna like this, Ilse thought.

The sky was clear and open, and Ilse could see the stars no matter what direction she looked in. There were stars above her head, stars to the side, and stars disappearing behind the mountains.

Ilse fell backwards into the soft grass, and snuggled in. *Father would've loved to come here with me,* Ilse thought. Ilse knew that if Father were here, he would've told her a story about the scenery in front of them. She silently hoped he wasn't hurt, or in a camp.

What if he and Mother were at a death camp like Tante Gisela had said? Ilse shook the thought away.

Ilse stared at the stars, trying to find a constellation that might tell a new story– one where Father and Mother were safe and by her side.

The First Summer

June 1939, Maria Alm, Austria

The sun was extra bright Ilse's first morning in Maria Alm. Hues of red, orange, and yellow rose from behind the mountains surrounding the town. *Was it really that beautiful, or was it just me being out in the country for the first time?* Ilse wondered. She didn't know for sure. Ilse was sitting downstairs in the main area of Tante Gisela's home. Well, *her* home now.

The wooden rafters crossed in so many directions to support the triangular roof. A chandelier hung from the centermost rafter. A moose's head was anchored above the fireplace, devoid of wood, and that entire wall was made of stone. Antique rugs covered the dark-stained wood that was all over the house. The walls were in the same color and material. Tante Gisela didn't have much artwork like Frau Kofler, and she couldn't see any photographs. Tante Gisela did have walls and walls of books towards the right-side of the room. They were in so many different colors it was hard to not go over and touch each one. A couch faced the fireplace and two other armchairs were perpendicular to it. Ilse noticed an empty flowerpot sat in the middle. Across the room was her traditional dining room set, with seats for four.

Tante Gisela must be so lonely here, Ilse thought.

Ilse wondered what the town looked like. After all, things in the dark appear *much* more different to their appearance in the day. Ilse saw some hills in Salzburg, but none of the never-ending lakes and tall mountains like she had imagined. She surely wouldn't mind walking everywhere, but it *would* be nice to have a bike to get around. She'd have to ask Tante Gisela about that. Then again, Ilse did not want to spend too much of Tante Gisela's money. She felt guilty enough about having Tante Gisela taking her in.

Ilse heard soft steps coming from above, and she turned to see Tante Gisela covered in her baby pink bathrobe. She looked quite tall from this angle.

"Good morning, Tante Gisela," Ilse chimed. She still wasn't too sure on how to act around her. *What are we supposed to be like around each other?* Ilse wondered. It was extremely odd having to establish a dynamic with a new person after having been quite lonely for a few months.

"Good morning, Ilse," Tante Gisela replied. "Got anything in mind for today?"

Ilse shrugged, as Tante Gisela made her way into the kitchen. She filled two mugs with hot water.

"I quite like seeing the stars. I have to confess, I've never been in the country before," Ilse said.

Tante Gisela let out a hearty laugh. It sounded like wind chimes. "You can stargaze whenever you'd like," she said as she made her way to the coffee table. She sat down next to Ilse, handing her the mug.

Ilse sipped, feeling a nice bubble of warmth in her stomach.

"Thank you," Ilse said. "But I also wanted to know one more thing."

"Sure, ask me anything." Tante Gisela said.

"Are there any people my age?" Ilse asked. "I don't want to live *completely* alone while I'm here."

Tante Gisela was sipping her water, but she quickly swallowed to answer.

"*That's* what I wanted to mention! Ilse, the children play outside at the schoolyard almost every day of the summer. You can make friends there, I'm sure. It's mostly younger children, but there's people your age you can play with."

That sounded quite nice. "In Vienna, we didn't really have a schoolyard. Playdates, based on the few I had when I was little, were mostly fancy dolls and dollhouses in some closed up apartment," Ilse said.

Tante Gisela nodded thoughtfully. "I can tell you it's way different here. My sister must've told you how everyone knows everyone here. Somehow, we've managed to share the same mindset: simplicity. We're a simple town. Nothing fancy. You'll be friends with everyone in no time," she said.

Ilse smiled. "Great! Now, I don't have many summer clothes with me…" Ilse said, trailing off.

Tante Gisela waved her hand at Ilse. "I sent for clothes from the village shop months ago when Frau Kofler and I discussed plans for you to come," she said. "I knew it would happen eventually. Go upstairs, look in the closet."

Ilse dashed upstairs, and she threw open her closet doors. Tante Gisela soon followed.

There were so many beautiful clothes. Some were for summer, some for fall, and some for winter. Ilse could tell a few pairs of pants and shirts were new, but a lot of the stack was used and worn. She didn't care. It felt nice to have something new!

Ilse threw her arms around Tante Gisela. "*Thank you, thank you, THANK YOU!*" Ilse squealed.

Tante Gisela patted Ilse's shoulder. "No problem, Ilse. I'll leave you to pick a pair?" she asked. "I'm going to lock the main door, so go out the side door when you leave, alright?"

Ilse nodded. "Where can I get lunch?"

"The inn has a restaurant," she said. "It's really a café, but it has all the food you could ever need. So, come by when you get hungry, alright?"

Ilse nodded.

"It's in the town center. You can't miss it. You *will* be alright, right? Should I give you a tour of the town? Of course, there isn't much to *tour–*"

"Don't worry, Tante Gisela. I'll be okay. How about I change, and I'll meet you at the inn? It'll give me a chance to explore a little."

She nodded. "Yes, of course."

After Tante Gisela had left, Ilse put on a faded blue plaid dress and tied her hair into two pigtails. The dress was definitely old material, but it looked quite cute. Ilse smoothed out the dress. This would be the *perfect* first impression for everyone in town!

Ilse went straight down the hill, turned the bend, then continued a downhill slope. Ilse walked straight past the row of homes to the left and went into the center of town. It was mostly empty, with some people walking here and there. Ilse glanced around the square.

The closed pizzeria was the building Ilse saw yesterday, a small section of it projecting outwards. A bakery was next to it, and Ilse could smell cinnamon and dough in the air. There was a dress shop, a children's boutique, and a men's store. Small and simple, but enough. Ilse could see the top of the church behind the buildings. The inn had its porch lights on, so Ilse went up the steps and hauled open the door.

The room was unusually large, especially for what Ilse expected to be a small cafe, and people of all sorts were moving around. A long bar was set up along one end of the room and it had all types of delicacies. Bread rolls, cut ham, sausages, boiled eggs, Danish buns, and so much more filled the back of the room. People were mostly sipping on coffee or orange juice.

A lady in a clean suit approached Ilse, standing behind a desk.

"Good morning, welcome to the Maria Alm Inn Café! Your total fee will be 82 schillings." She was extremely cheery.

Ilse spotted Tante Gisela in a blue dress, standing and talking to an elderly couple at the table. She waved her arms subtly, trying to catch Tante Gisela's attention. She briefly glanced up, and upon seeing Ilse, made her way over.

"I'm with my aunt, Tante Gisela," Ilse replied. She uncomfortably brushed past the hostess and walked to Tante Gisela.

"Herr Weiss, Frau Weiss, I would like you to meet my niece." Her warm hands found their way to Ilse's shoulders. "Meet Ilse Kofler, Therese's girl."

Ilse felt uncomfortable using her new name, but played along for her own sake. Ilse smiled graciously, nodding her head.

"Good morning, Herr Weiss. You as well, Frau Weiss. It is a pleasure to stay with Tante Gisela, and I am looking forward to meeting more of the town." Ilse stepped back, careful to not say too much.

The woman grinned. "She's got such good manners. I had no idea Therese had a daughter. What brings her here?" This was Ilse's cue to back out.

"I'm going to grab something to eat," Ilse said to Tante Gisela, and she motioned her hands at the long table of food.

"Therese is doing fine. We exchanged some letters months ago and met up once. She is sending Ilse to me for some time, because of the violence in the city." The rest of the conversation trailed into the distance.

Ilse quickly ate at a table in the back of the room, then checked the clock. 9:32. Ilse walked up to Tante Gisela, who was now standing at the hostess table.

Ilse cleared her throat. "How can I get to the schoolyard?"

Tante Gisela looked happy to see Ilse and walked her out to the porch.

"Go straight across, through the two buildings over there. Make a right, past the church and it should be straight ahead." Tante Gisela smiled, brushing her fingers through her hair. "You'll do great."

Ilse laughed, jumping down the stairs and running into the center of the town, to the opening between the two buildings. People were filtering in, sitting at tables in the cafes around the square. Ilse could see lights coming on, and the town seemed like an oasis of sorts. *Why was there so much space between the buildings?* Ilse wondered, thinking of Vienna. She could smell nature everywhere.

Ilse skipped through the gap between the buildings. She hadn't looked at what they were for. Once she came out the other side, there was a thin, simple wire fence alongside the dirt path behind the building. It was fairly low and stringy, so essentially useless. To the right, Ilse saw the church. It was a little way away, so she skipped the way over. Some other children were walking on the path, so Ilse slowed down and straightened her outfit. Hopefully, they would like her.

The school building was the size of two large houses, with the traditional wooden outing and balcony Ilse had seen in all the other homes. The only way Ilse could tell that it was a school was the open field behind it, with balls and jump ropes scattered around. The younger children were standing in a group near the building, while the older kids were huddled in their own circle. The younger kids were a group of about fifteen, while the older ones were a group of just five people. Ilse walked stealthily to the younger children's group and found an open spot in the circle to stand in.

A pretty girl with brown, curly hair was talking to the group. She had hazel eyes and was only about five feet tall. Everyone else was at least two inches taller than her. The children tuned into her and what she was saying.

"*Nein!* We are to love one another, no matter what." The girl looked exasperated and shot a death stare at a boy across from her in the bubble.

The boy looked very similar to her, except he was the tallest of the group. His hair and eyes matched hers.

Ilse wondered what they were talking about. Ilse wanted to fit in, so she decided she would go along with the majority. Most of the kids were younger than nine, as far as Ilse could tell, so maybe they would look up to her as an older girl.

"You're so naive, Greta. I took one of Father's papers," the boy said while rummaging his hand through his pockets. Ilse moved closer, almost standing right next to the girl, who she presumed to be Greta.

A folded up, singular sheet of thin paper came from his pocket. He unfolded it, and it looked to be a newspaper.

"Here, read what it says." The boy cleared his throat. "The Jews are after world dominance. They use monetary power and financial gain against others." He closed the paper triumphantly.

Ilse nearly gagged. In Vienna, everyone talked about Jews. In Maria Alm, everyone talked about Jews. *Why can't I escape it?* Ilse thought.

Greta rolled her eyes. "Georg, you're so gullible. This is untrue. Mother said so."

The dynamic between the two of them pointed to the fact that they were siblings.

"You're lying to everyone. Father said all the Jews in the country were deported to camps and killed already." Georg scoffed, turning and heading to the field.

Ilse's heart cried out in pain. *Is that what happened to my parents?* Ilse wondered. Her stomach curled. Right now, she wanted to cry into Father's arms, but she didn't even know where he was. The crowd split apart.

Ilse walked up to Greta. She knew she had to be confident to make new friends, and who better than Greta?

"I heard what you said, and I agree." Ilse had to say it. She couldn't bite her tongue anymore.

Greta turned around, looking surprised. "What?"

"I agree with you. Your brother is being absurd."

She smiled. "He's ridiculous. He repeats everything our father says about Jewish people, without actually knowing what he's saying." She rolled her eyes.

Ilse giggled. "My name is Ilse."

"I'm Greta." She twisted her finger around one of her curls. "We're glad to have you here. It's quite lonely being the only twelve-year-old in the group. Other than Georg," she said, rolling her eyes again.

"I noticed. Most of the people in the group you were standing with are quite young."

She laughed. "They are more like little sisters and brothers, compared to classmates. Everyone's parents know each other. It's a small town," she said matter-of-factly. "Speaking of which, who are your parents?"

Ilse hoped she didn't know too much about Tante Gisela.

"I'm staying with my aunt. Gisela Kofler," Ilse said. "She runs the inn."

Greta nodded fast. "I know Fraulein Gisela," she said. "My mother will go to her inn to eat sometimes, and they are good friends."

Ilse was excited to meet someone like her. She seemed open and caring. It helped that she wasn't hateful towards Jewish people either.

"My mother is her sister, Therese Kofler." It felt abnormal to call some who was supposed to be my mother by her first name. "My father and her are back at our flat in Vienna, waiting for me to come home." At least, that's how Ilse wished it was.

"So, what types of things are you interested in?" Greta asked. They were slowly beginning to drift from the main group.

"I like to read and learn about stars," Ilse said. She didn't want to seem to boring, but she wanted to be honest. "It's my first time coming to the country, too. So far I like it."

Greta laughed. "And I've never been to the city. I like singing and playing outside," she said.

"I actually haven't seen much of town. Tante Gisela is working at the inn, so she decided to let me explore for a little," Ilse said.

"Well, I wouldn't mind accompanying you around," Greta said. "We can play with the others another day. Let's make your first day in Maria Alm the best!"

Greta turned to the group of children. She clapped three times, and instantly got their attention.

"Everyone, welcome Ilse Kofler! She is the niece of Fraulein Gisela from the inn. Say hello to Ilse!"

All the children chanted. "Hello Ilse!"

Ilse smiled and waved to them, even the little ones. They were so cute.

"I'm going to show Ilse around town. Everyone be good, alright?"

The children murmured "yes" and "okay" a few times, then went back to play.

Greta and Ilse walked back down the dirt road, right up to the church.

"This is our church. It's much more beautiful on the inside," Greta said. "Fraulein Ingrid, our teacher, said it was built in 1300… isn't that fascinating?"

The outside was one of the most grandiose churches Ilse had ever seen. From where they were standing, the needle-sharp steeple towered above the mountains. The building was made of smooth white and gray stone, and had a large bronze clock in the front. It looked even better in the day than it did at night.

"It's so beautiful," Ilse said breathlessly.

Greta smiled. "I know, right? You'd expect a modest church for a town like ours. Did you know that it's the largest in Salzburg?"

"The city doesn't have a bigger church?" Ilse asked.

"Nope. Okay, moving on…" Greta said.

Greta and Ilse walked down the dirt road then made a left between the two buildings. Then, they were in the town square.

"Straight ahead is, you know it, the Kofler Inn. Owned and operated by your aunt. Just across is the pizzeria operated by Lorenzo and Giulia Valerio from Naples. I have absolutely no idea why they moved here, but they bring the best pizza recipe of Italy with them. It's quite popular. You'll have to come with me some time," Greta said.

"I will," Ilse replied. "My aunt told me about more of the places that are a bit of a ways out. We can see them later, right?"

Greta rolled her eyes playfully. "*Of course* you will! We'll save the rest for later. It's only June, after all."

Ilse was super grateful to have made a friend, especially one as exciting as Greta. She had so much energy that it balanced out Ilse's lack of it.

The pair walked to the fountain in the center of the square, and Ilse ran her hands through the cool water, dripping some over her forehead. The sun was blazing down on the square, and Ilse felt so tired because of it. Greta was looking off into space, but then out of a sudden she looked mischievous.

Seconds later, both her hands were in the water and she splashed what seemed like bucketful of water right into Ilse's face! Sure, it was blazing hot but Ilse didn't expect to get soaked!

"*Greta!*" Ilse squealed. "I'm going to get you back!"

Ilse splashed her with another bucketful back.

Greta let out a screech. "*Ilse!*"

After the splash match, the soaked girls rushed to the inn. Ilse dashed to the door, and none other than Tante Gisela was standing right at the front. Ilse could tell she wanted to laugh as soon as she saw Ilse, but she held it in.

"You girls wait here," Tante Gisela said, walking down the hall.

Greta and Ilse stood, dripping water onto the beautiful wooden floor. Tante Gisela returned with towels.

Greta immediately grabbed hers and started drying off the floor they had made wet. Tante Gisela laughed again.

"Greta, you need not worry. I have a deep cleaner coming in-", she glanced at the clock, "-twelve minutes. I schedule him once a month, and today happens to be the day. You girls want anything to eat?"

Bundled in the towels, the girls smiled at each other.

"I think that's all we need for now," Ilse said.

When Tante Gisela returned later on that night, Ilse decided to try and express her gratitude in a way Tante Gisela hadn't seen before. She was always working, busy or exhausted, so Ilse planned a little treat for her.

Tante Gisela came in through the side door, and the second she came in, Ilse grabbed her wrist.

"Ilse, what are you–?"

"Shh, I have to show you something."

Ilse ran up the hill, and Tante Gisela was panting right behind her. When they got to the top Tante Gisela tried to say something, but Ilse gently shushed her and walked farther back until the only thing they could see were stars.

"Wow," Tante Gisela muttered. "Ilse, they're so gorgeous."

"Lay down." Ilse said.

"What?" Tante Gisela asked.

"It's better when you lay down." Ilse tumbled back into the grass, soaking in the fresh night air.

Tante Gisela laid back, and gazed into the sky. "You would think that I would know about this stargazing spot in my own backyard. I have to confess I've never been into nature much," she said.

"What?" Ilse yelped. "You have all this and you've never enjoyed it?"

She shook her head. "I think I'm too focused on my work. It is nice sitting back and relaxing sometimes."

Tante Gisela sighed. "But these stars are really beautiful, Ilse. Thank you for showing me."

Ilse gazed until Tante Gisela fell asleep, and she smiled at the sky.

This summer was off to a good start.

School

September 1939, Maria Alm, Austria

September was here before Ilse knew it. There was a slight chill in the air that breezed by ever so often, reminding her that summer was coming to a close.

The first day of school was today, and surprisingly, Ilse wasn't nervous. She had played with Greta and the other children over the summer, and she was so much closer to Tante Gisela now. Everything was going great. Maybe moving to Maria Alm wasn't a bad decision after all.

After Ilse dragged herself down the stairs, she found that Tante Gisela had left her a note saying she would be at the inn until late tonight.

Ilse grabbed her schoolbag, an old one of Tante Gisela's, and stuck some books inside. Ilse stole a notepad and a pen in the kitchen. Books for math, language and science would probably be at the school. She went out the side door, walked around the house, and through the town.

Ilse made her way to the schoolyard, where she found Greta. All the children were dressed very informally, some in trousers and some in colorful dresses. In Vienna, they had to wear *uniforms*!

"Greta, I probably should've asked this sooner, but what are our classes like? How many rooms are there?"

"They split us up by our age. It's slightly different every year," Greta said. "We're going to the church today."

What was she talking about? Why did we have to go to church? Ilse wondered. *What would we do?* Ilse was too scared to ask, but she knew she would have to play along with whatever went on.

A sudden clanging came from the bell tower connected to the church. A large opening in the shape of a window was cut so that you could see the person ringing the bell. A young boy had latched himself onto the long rope connected to the bell and was swinging back and forth.

Greta tapped Ilse's shoulder. "This means we are to go inside and start lessons."

Ilse followed the rest of the children inside the school.

School was easy. At least that was one less thing to worry about. Since there weren't very many children, the children were grouped up into age groups– ten-, eleven- and twelve-year-olds took the same classes. There were only about eight children in Ilse's class.

Starting with the youngest, there were the ten-year-olds: Mario, Flavia, and Emil. Mario and Flavia were the children of the pizza restaurant owners, and they were carbon copies of them. Mario inherited his father's thin, noodle-like body, while Flavia looked plump and rosy, like their mother. They were the gnats of the classroom— "How did the first person to milk a cow know where to squeeze?", "What happens if you eat raw pasta?" These were the least of their stupid questions. Ilse constantly wanted to slap them. Emil was a little blond boy that had rows of razor-sharp teeth. He hardly made a peep and just stared into space most of the day.

The eleven-year-olds weren't quite as unbearable. There was only one boy named Friedrich. Friedrich was a smart and eloquent boy and lived on the opposite hill with his father, Greta said. Ilse didn't have much of a problem with him. He had jet-black hair and a tight smile. The girls in the group, however, weren't quite as good as him. Antonia and Elisabeth were the inseparable best friends, though it seemed to Ilse that their friendship was more bonded on gossiping and pranking the younger children.

Ilse's group, the twelve-year-olds, weren't significantly better. There was Georg, the snarky Nazi sympathizer. He was Greta's twin. How could two people of the same blood be so different? Ilse wanted to laugh when she thought about it.

Greta watched the younger children and played with them. She was smart and excelled in all subjects. Then, there was Ilse. Ilse Kofler, a Catholic girl from Vienna. What did she like? Nature and constellations. When she thought about it, Ilse found herself to be quite boring.

The teacher was a slim, pretty woman named Fraulein Ingrid, and she had the most beautiful strawberry blond hair Ilse had ever seen. It shimmered in the light, depending on where she stepped. Her hair was done in a classic lace-braided bun, similar to what Mother would do on Ilse's hair. She had a light, flowery voice and wore spectacles.

Fraulein Ingrid worked on a basic math curriculum for the eleven-year-olds, so Ilse had time to let her mind wander.

Ilse spotted a pile of books with Jesus on the cross on the teacher's desk. *Little Catholic,* the title said. She held in a laugh. *I wasn't so little, was I?* Ilse thought. Though she *did* wonder what was in the book.

Ilse glanced over at the table with the ten-year-olds. Fraulein Ingrid was so consumed in teaching them the lesson, Ilse was sure she wouldn't notice her move. After all, Ilse finished the problems Fraulein Ingrid had given her. Greta and Georg were still working.

Ilse scooted her chair backwards, nonchalantly leaning, so her hand could reach the stack of books. She grabbed at the pile, quickly pulling the book to her chest. Ilse looked around. No one made a peep.

Ilse opened the book to the index, where illustrations of goats, birds and fields filled the pages. She scanned the chapters.

Would I need to tell the priest anything in the book? Would I say any anything at all to the priest when we went to the church? A myriad of questions were spinning through her head.

Ilse was curious, but not scared. After everything she'd been through, she knew she could do anything.

The class stood outside of the church. The sun was out, which made the fall winds a little more bearable. Everyone was waiting for the church bells to ring.

"Once the bells ring, we'll be able to go inside. Instead of theology class, we are going to confess our sins to a priest," Greta said.

"Oh, that's just saying what we did wrong," Ilse said.

"Like always," Greta said.

That didn't seem too bad to Ilse. *Nobody would know I wasn't Catholic if I just said what I did wrong,* Ilse thought.

The bells rang, and Fraulein Ingrid yanked the door open.

The inside of the church was absolutely grand, with ceilings seeming to stretch to the mountains and rows and rows of endless pews. A large, velvet drape was behind a cross. It was juniper colored, and extremely long. Ilse could smell warm pine with notes of citrus and spice in the air. It felt like she had opened the pages of an ancient book and it had come to life. A marble table held a small row of candles and some folded cloths.

A spiky, round object was on the table, but it looked like a sun and its rays from a distance.

Ilse turned to Greta. "What is that on the table?" Ilse whispered.

She leaned in to Ilse's ear. "The monstrance?" Greta dipped her finger in a glass of water on the pew and made the sign of the cross. Ilse followed, dipping her finger into the cool water.

The school group sat in the row in the very back, next to a small room with a thick, swimming glass and wood door. Mario, being at the end of the row, stood up first. He knelt, making the sign of the cross, and turned, walking towards the door. It closed slowly, swinging back and forth a few times.

The rest of the class removed a set of kneelers stored under the pews, sliding them out discreetly.

Even the gossip girls, Elisabeth and Antonia had stopped their banter. Ilse slide out her kneeler.

Mario, Flavia, and Friedrich had brought rosaries, and were slowly moving their fingers around the beads. Ilse folded her hands and bent her head down. This way, no one could see her.

Ilse was the second person in line on the way to church, which meant she would be second-to-last for going into the room. That was for confessing, right?

Soon, Mario came out and knelt back down. Ilse saw his lips move for a few minutes, then he leaned back onto the pew. Flavia had left as soon as he came back. Ilse made a note of this. As soon as one person came back, the next person could go. Did the priest need to know if you prayed after? How would he know?

One by one, the entire row was sitting back on the pew in silence. Friedrich, Emil, Antonia, and Elisabeth had gone, leaving Ilse and Greta to go. Georg had just left for the confessional, and a few of the people were still finishing their prayers.

Suddenly, Ilse's brain sparked. If she had to confess something, that means she had to list everything she did wrong. Oh no. *How long will this take?* Ilse wondered.

Ilse racked her brains. *What have I done wrong so far?* Ilse thought.

Ilse complained to Mother a lot in the apartment. That could be her first one.

Ilse kept thinking, and suddenly it hit her.

Ilse had lied to an officer. Ilse had lied about her religion.

But surely it didn't matter. It was for her safety, after all. Ilse bit her lip. *What kind of lies were okay, and which ones weren't?* Ilse wondered.

Georg exited, and Ilse stood up, swallowing the lump in her throat.

Ilse walked around the pew and opened the door. It swung back and forth a few times, and she put her hand on the handle to slow it down and close it completely. She didn't want to let anyone else know her secrets.

An old man sat on a chair at the back of the room. He had a kind, relaxed expression on his face, but his eyes were closed. To Ilse, the man had a meditative and serene presence. At the same time, he appeared shrunken and flaccid. His large, rounded spectacles were placed delicately on the end of his nose. The cassock he wore was black, with a little white collar. There were so many buttons on it, going down to his ankles. He was a priest.

"Sit, child." His voice was deep and drawn out, and Ilse was scared that someone outside would hear. Ilse calmed herself, remembering he had done this to the children before her, and she hadn't heard anything.

Ilse quickly plopped herself onto the chair directly in front of him, squirming in discomfort.

Ilse's palms began to sweat. She ran a mental check of the confession procedure through her head. But when Ilse heard the priest's voice again, she immediately calmed.

"You may begin your confession." His eyes were two different colors, one light blue and one light green.

The priest closed his eyes, leaning back slightly.

Ilse swallowed, hoping he wouldn't hear it. She made the sign of the cross, since she had seen Friedrich do it.

What did I have to do next? Ilse wondered.

"Father, I forget what to say next."

"Repeat this phrase. 'Bless me Father, for I have sinned. This is my Confession.' Tell me when your last confession was as well."

"Bless me Father, for I have sinned. This is my"— Ilse's voice cracked—" confession."

The priest opened both his eyes, still looking calm. "Child, how old are you?"

"Thirteen years old," Ilse whispered hoarsely. She was so scared he would judge her.

"And may I ask, is this your first time at this church?" He spoke slowly, and calmly. It felt like a wave of serotonin had rushed over Ilse.

"At this one? Yes. It's my first time at Church," Ilse said. She tried her best to continue on. "My first sin is that I was disrespectful to my mother. I complained to her a lot."

The priest nodded.

"My second sin is that I lied to, erm, an important person. That's all," Ilse said.

The priest nodded, and made the sign of the cross over Ilse. He said a prayer, and Ilse thanked him quickly.

The class left the church soon after. Ilse thought about lying all the way home. *Was it bad to tell a lie, even though it was for my own sake?* Ilse wondered.

Now, Ilse was starting to notice all the little lies she told. She felt like a bad kid.

Greta and Ilse made their way to the town center when class ended. The fall air was fresh on Ilse's skin, and everything was so new.

"Let's go to the inn," Ilse said as they passed the fountain. "Tante Gisela will let us hang out in the café."

Greta smiled. "That would be nice. I haven't finished my math work," she said.

The pair went inside, and Ilse found Tante Gisela standing at the welcome desk. She glanced up.

"Afternoon, Ilse." Then, she looked down. Right after, she glanced back up. "Why hello Greta," she said. "Nice to see you when you aren't dripping wet."

Greta giggled. "I'm glad to not stain your floors as well. Can we work in the café?"

Tante Gisela nodded, beckoning us to the empty room. *Why wasn't it full of people like before?* Ilse wondered.

Greta immediately sat at a table and pulled out a math problem set.

Ilse went up to Tante Gisela, who was filing papers. "Why is it slow today? Back when I first came here, there were so many customers."

Tante Gisela sighed, resting her head on her hand. "Business has been a little slow. It's only afternoon right now. I hope dinner will pick up the slack from the morning," she said.

"I'm so sorry about that. What can I do to help?" Ilse asked.

"Go study and play with Greta. Don't worry about this. Did you want anything to eat?" Tante Gisela asked.

"We're good for now," Ilse said. She felt quite bad. *How could I ask her for more food when she was already having trouble at the inn?* Ilse thought. She didn't want to take any more of Tante Gisela's money than she had to.

Ilse went back to Greta, and she was staring hard at her paper.

Ilse laughed. "Greta, what are you doing?"

"I can't figure out the answer. I thought that perhaps if I stared at it for long enough the answer would come to me," Greta said.

"Don't be silly," Ilse said. "Let me look at the problem."

Greta moved aside, and Ilse looked at the equation. Surprisingly, it was super simple. All the problems Greta didn't know how to do, Ilse knew how.

But Greta seemed so smart at school! She was so fun, fast and quick to think.

Maybe Ilse was letting the idea of Greta being the perfect friend overcome the fact that she was human, just like Ilse.

"No worries, Greta. All you have to do is divide by 2 and double it," Ilse explained.

Greta squinted, scribbled some numbers, then circled her answer.

Ilse glanced. "Perfect! Apply the same theory to the rest of the paper," Ilse said.

Greta smiled. "Thanks for your help, Ilse."

"Anytime," Ilse replied.

The Boy in the Barn

November 1939, Maria Alm, Austria

The next few months in Maria Alm passed fairly uneventfully. Tante Gisela promised to take Ilse tobogganing on the hill when it snowed, and they were making hot chocolate at the inn. Ilse was beginning to settle into the fall season in Maria Alm. Every night, Ilse went out to look at the stars.

Whenever Tante Gisela had finished stirring her nightly tea, and Ilse heard her footsteps diminish into the staircase, Ilse would take her opportunity and to escape to the outdoors. Now she wasn't *escaping* Tante Gisela– it was just nice to have some alone time. Sometimes, Tante Gisela accompanied Ilse, but it was quite rare, especially since she was always exhausted after a long day's work. Ilse thought of it like their own special thing, and something to look forward to every now and then. However, tonight was going to be all hers.

Clink. Tante Gisela's spoon clacked against the ceramic, and the steam come to a halt from her cup. Her slippers were worn and fraying, and definitely a size too small. Her robe looked just the same as Frau Kofler's. Although she was younger than Frau Kofler, she appeared older in some ways. Something about her just *seemed* sullen and sad. She didn't exactly *look* it on the outside.

Ilse was sitting on the couch, pretending to be immersed in a book she found on the shelves. Ilse couldn't think clearly with Tante Gisela standing right in the kitchen, and she wanted to get outside as soon as possible. All day at school, she'd been decorating pinecones with little children, and then when she went to the inn for a drink, Ilse found it completely crowded and full of people. She just needed a *little* bit of silence.

"Enjoying your book?" Tante Gisela asked.

Ilse glanced up. Tante Gisela was rinsing off her spoon and setting it on the drying rack.

Ilse quickly scanned the cover. "Doctor Doolittle is definitely one of my favorite characters," she lied.

That felt odd to Ilse as soon as she said it. Ever since her first confession at the church, Ilse had started monitoring all the little lies she told. She felt guilty about it. Ilse didn't know she lied that much, or that it even mattered. But inside her heart, Ilse could feel that it wasn't right, no matter what religion she was.

Overall, living in the countryside was better than ever, and Ilse felt free of the troubles in the world. There weren't raids or soldiers or violence here. After the little incident with Georg at the school, Ilse hadn't heard much about the war. Tante Gisela skimmed over the topic, and the schoolchildren seemed to remain oblivious. Ilse couldn't decide if this was a good or bad thing.

Things were a little too quiet, a little too peaceful. Sure, Ilse was safe from the chaos in Vienna but she couldn't help but wonder how her parents were. Ilse had hoped and hoped someone would help them, but what could she do? They were taken so fast.

Tante Gisela walked to the stairs, carefully balancing her tea on a plate. "Goodnight, Ilse," she called out. "Put the lights out when you're going to sleep."

Ilse turned and smiled. "Goodnight, Tante Gisela."

Tante Gisela disappeared into the darkness.

Ilse heard a door shut, and she tiptoed over to the closet. Ilse carefully turned the doorknob, careful to not make a noise. She grabbed the candle that shelit for her reading. After all, it wouldn't hurt to bring it outside, just in case it was too dark. Ilse grabbed a blanket from the couch and wrapped it around her shoulder. She figured she could use the extra heat.

Once Ilse got outside, she ran up the hill, which seemed especially steep today. Once on the peak, Ilse began to run backward, until she was *absolutely* sure no one in the town would see Ilse. This time, she went farther back on the plain than she ever had before.

A small barn was enclosed in a patch of trees farther up the hill. Ilse hadn't seen it where she usually laid, but it was a nice sight for her eyes. Maria Alm looked practically the same in all of its streets and turns, but she hadn't actually seen a barn before. Ilse went up closer to the barn and lay against one of the trees.

The air smelled fresh. Leaves were falling off the trees. A cool gust of wind blew in her face every minute or so. The town, far, far ahead, was just specks of deep yellow and brown.

Stars continued to pop up and fill the sky, like sprouting flowers. Gazing into the dark blue, Ilse realized that it was the only part of her world that hadn't changed. The vastness felt homely. And no matter many years that had passed, Ilse continued to see each night sky as a new gift for herself.

In Vienna, snow piled on thick across the streets and building tops. Men with shovels could be spotted from the living room window in the early snowy mornings, hacking away at the ground. Mother would normally walk around, buying woolen hats or mittens for friends. She would buy all sorts of sweets, decorations and ceramics for her family in Poland. Ilse would sneak a pack or two of the chocolates, of course. Winters were so different.

A sudden realization overcame Ilse. *How did I remember the details?* Ilse wondered. Small parts of her identity were beginning to slip from her mind, and it had only been a few months since her life changed. Ilse responded at once to Ilse Kofler, never giving a second thought to Ilse Stadler. She often pushed the thoughts of her parents out of her mind before she could process it and cry. For some reason, coming outside to look at the stars helped her to think better.

Achoo!

Ilse's eyes popped out of her head and she froze. *Was that a sneeze?* Ilse wondered.

A rustle came from behind her. She slowly turned, peering behind her.

The only thing behind Ilse was the barn.

Maybe the word "barn" was a stretch. Sure, it was *shaped* like a barn, but the red paint was faded and chipped, and it was only a few yards taller than Ilse.

Ilse stepped up, careful to not make any noise. The soft grass still held the snow from Thursday's fall, which making Ilse's footsteps visible.

Ilse put her hand to the door. After a brief hesitation, she tried to slide it to the side. For some reason, it wouldn't budge.

Sniff.

Ilse's heart beat faster. *What was in the barn?* Ilse wondered.

She stalked around, looking at the other end of the barn.

There was a similar door on that end too. Ilse wondered what would happen if she tried to open it. Ilse pushed it, jumping back.

The light of the moon bouncing off the snow illuminated the barn.

The inside of the barn was nearly pitch black, but Ilse could make out a few things with her candle. A stack of gardening tools was lined up to the right, along with some old tubing. Oddly enough, a dirty horse saddle was thrown to the back right corner. Ilse's heart skipped a beat when she was what was to her left.

A small, blond boy was huddled in the corner, his hand covering his mouth. Ilse could see tears leaking out of his eyes, practically begging her to not hurt him. Ilse's heart softened, and she knelt down next to him. He was covering his shaking body with the saddle pad.

"Hello." Ilse waved, smiling gently. "What's your name?"

The boy wiped his eyes, looking rather apprehensive.

"I'm Ilse. I'm not here to hurt you," Ilse said sweetly.

Once he saw Ilse wasn't a threat, he relaxed a little. Ilse kept her voice soft. "What are you doing in the barn? Why don't we get you on home?" She extended her arm to him. He buried his face in his palms.

"I don't live here." His voice was high-pitched, and Ilse could tell he was a lot younger than her. He smelled like old hay, and his body was shaking. His teeth chattered, and his cheeks were bright pink.

"What?" Ilse asked. Ilse took off her blanket and wrapped it around him.

"I can't trust you," the boy said shakily.

Ilse sat down on the rough flooring, leaning forward. She extended her pinky.

"I promise I won't do anything to hurt you." Ilse said, looking him in the eyes.

They locked fingers for a brief moment. He pulled away, adjusting the blanket to cover his shoulders.

"My name's Leon. I'm seven. A soldier came to my house today, and I had to escape out the back window. I fell into the Salzach."

Ilse smiled. The Salzach is the river that runs through the middle of Salzburg. But then, a realization hit her. Leon must be Jewish. Why else would he run from a soldier?

Father's words echoed in Ilse's mind.

"First thing, never let on you are Jewish. Nobody can know this. From now on, you are to be Roman Catholic. Does this make sense?"

Ilse told Father yes. Alas, she made a promise that she couldn't keep.

"Are you Jewish?" Ilse asked Leon sweetly.

Leon seemed to squirm even more. He wrinkled his nose.

"Why do you need to know?" Leon questioned.

"I'm Jewish too," Ilse said, a small smile forming on her lips.

Leon scrunched his lips together. "Yes, I am Jewish. Technically. It's so boring up here."

Ilse laughed. "Leon, boring is what you make of it. How about this? You tell me your story; I'll tell you mine. So, you can figure out why I'm here right now, and we can be friends."

Ilse had big and distant dreams of finding her parents and moving back into her apartment, but not one of finding another Jew. Yet finding another person in hiding gave Ilse hope. Maybe she would get out of here soon. Maybe they could *both* get out of here.

"So, Leon. How'd you get in this run-down barn in the middle of nowhere?"

Ilse's mouth was agape. "What?"

Leon laughed. "Yes, it's true!" He squealed.

Leon had left from Salzburg early this morning, when he heard banging on his front door and a few Nazis barged in. At least that's what he inferred from the boot clicks and German accents.

The first thing Leon did was run to his window, which faced the river. He unlocked it and perched on the windowsill for a few moments. The second he heard the footsteps in the halls, he jumped, pulling the window shut as he jumped out.

That explained the damp pajamas he was in.

"And then, I swam across the Salzach. It was freezing. I was shaking and shivering the entire way over. The soldiers didn't see me, probably because they didn't think to look out the window."

Ilse leaned against the wall. She could see her breath in the teeth-chattering cold air. It was beginning to get light outside.

"I had no place to go. The people on our end of the bank know who my family is. There was no escaping them. Mamma told me, many months ago, that she feared the Nazis would take me away."

To Ilse, it was funny that someone as young as Leon would have to deal with something like this. He was only seven! *It's not fair that he has to worry about surviving right now,* Ilse thought.

Leon fumbled with the blanket. "I didn't think it would actually happen."

Ilse could see specks of orange and yellow in the cracks of the barn doors. She stood up, brushing the dirt off Tante Gisela's coat.

"Leon, I have to go back home."

He pouted. "I'm hungry, Ilse."

"I have school, and honestly, I have no what time it is. I'll come back in a few hours with some food and blankets. Alright?" Ilse said.

Leon pulled the blanket close to him. "See you, Ilse," he said softly.

Ilse smiled, walking to the door. She pushed it open. Ilse waved to Leon, and he closed his eyes into deep slumber.

Ilse returned back home as soon as she got out of school. Dark circles rounded her eyes, and Tante Gisela was concerned.

"Ilse, are you sick?" she had asked.

"No, I just had trouble sleeping." That was code for "No, I discovered a Jewish boy in the barn out back." Ilse grimaced. She had lied *again*.

Greta wanted her to come over to play, and Ilse had to turn her down. Ilse hoped Greta didn't think something was wrong with her. After all, they were becoming best friends, and Ilse didn't want her obligation to Leon to get in the way of that.

"Another day?" Greta had called to Ilse, as they parted directions on the dirt road behind the town square.

"Another day!" Ilse yelled back.

Ilse ran down the path between the two buildings, darting past the fountain, and up the steps of the cafe. She peeked through the glass, and saw that the hostess wasn't at her station. Ilse threw her backpack onto a chair on the porch and snuck inside.

Ilse ran to the serving table and she took a plate. There was hardly anything there but leftovers from the morning breakfast. Ilse took some bread and butter, ham and hot cocoa in a mug.

Ilse walked surely, but calmly, down the road, up the hill, and across the grass where she spotted the tree patch. *How did I not notice the barn in the first place?* Ilse wondered.

"Leon, Leon!" Ilse called.

She went to the back door, kicking the door with her foot.

Moments later, it slid open, and Ilse saw the toothless smile of Leon. He grabbed the plate of food and started eating immediately.

Ilse smiled. Of course, that was the first thing on his mind.

"Let's go inside," Ilse whispered, "before anyone sees us."

He nodded, waving Ilse in, half-eaten piece in hand.

Ilse sat there for a few minutes while he gobbled down the rest of the food and as he chugged his lukewarm hot cocoa. Chocolate outlined his mouth, and crumbs of the bun stuck to his lip.

It seemed so unreal to Ilse. The fact that this little, messy boy had escaped a city full of

Nazis. Honestly, Ilse didn't think she would be too surprised if they showed up in Maria Alm one day.

"You have to finish telling me the story," Ilse said. "You've got some chocolate on your face."

Leon wiggled his tongue around the outer edges of his mouth.

"I want to finish my story now. Remember how I jumped out my window? I swam to the opposite bank. I was soaked, head to toe in blue pajamas. I knew I had to find a way out of the city. Anywhere in the country would be great, I just needed to get out. A horse drawn cart was coming down south, up near the bridge. The driver was a little old man, who had a toothy smile and a lot of trouble managing the cart. Despite that, he patted the empty spot on the carriage. He didn't actually say anything else. I don't know if the man actually understood what I said, because whenever I tried to ask where he was going, he gave a bellowing laugh and patted me on the back.

"We'd been on the ride for several hours, and it was beginning to get dark. We passed through the road on the bottom of this hill, and the man stopped the cart. He ushered me out, and pointed to this patch of trees."

Leon bit his fingernails. "I still wonder who he was."

Ilse chuckled. "Aren't you grateful for the kindness of strangers?"

He smiled, his dimples showing. "Definitely."

"Well, the only reason I'm even here today is *because* of the stranger in my apartment building," Ilse said.

Leon squinted. "Really?" he asked.

"Well, I'm from Vienna, and my neighbor's sister lives here. In Maria Alm. That's where you are, by the way. Anyways, I'm staying with her till I can go home safely," Ilse said.

Leon looked more confused. "But why don't you just stay in Vienna?"

"The Nazis tried to take me away from my parents. In the country, it's much harder to do that," Ilse explained. She wasn't even quite sure if that was true, but she felt that she had to give Leon *some* hope. At least he would have something to hold on to.

Christmas

December 1939, Maria Alm, Austria

Tante Gisela picked out the most beautiful Christmas tree. She got them from Meyer's, which was on the outskirts of town. According to her, Herr Meyer sold the best trees in the Salzburg state. She came a bit late to the game, on the last day of November, when all the families had taken the best trees. Yet Meyer still greeted Tante Gisela with the best pine tree in all of Maria Alm.

Herr Meyer also supplied the tree for the town center, and it was just as tall as the tallest building in the square. A group of twenty men had to carry it from his cart and lay it flat on the ground. All the families gathered round, putting on homemade cookies or tinsel decorations. At the end, Meyer would climb an enormous ladder and place the star on top. It truly was a beautiful sight.

Ilse never did many community activities in Vienna. Her family didn't even have a tree in the apartment. Maria Alm had a lot more experiences, for sure. All the Catholic kids would get gifts from St. Nikolaus, but Ilse didn't believe in him. She'd never seen him for herself, after all.

"Ilse, is this your first Catholic Christmas?" Tante Gisela asked.

Ilse snapped back to the present. "Pretty much. We didn't ever decorate or celebrate, other than visiting the Christmas market. But that's what everyone does, it doesn't matter what religion you are."

Ilse thought about Hannukah a little bit. She really didn't celebrate it. It was only a formality when they had family over, of course, but it still hurt to see little parts of who she was slowly go away. Tante Gisela expressed interest in having a Hannukah celebration at home, but Ilse quickly dismissed the idea. She didn't like to think about the past too much.

The living room was illuminated with several soft lights around the room. Tante Gisela had a teeny ladder she was standing on to decorate the tree. She brought out old boxes full of tinsel and fake gold decorations for the tree. "These were my great-grandmother's," she said admiringly. "I use them every year."

The box was full of every kind of ornament Ilse could imagine. Felt trees on aluminum hooks, metal trains, and plastic bulbs lined the boxes. They smelled dusty and old too.

Tante Gisela managed to acquire a small radio that played local broadcasts of the news, so they had that on as well.

Crescent cookies for the neighbors were baking in the oven. Tante Gisela told Ilse that she did this for the houses on the street beneath them every year. Ilse had met all of them. The grocer and dressmaker both lived down there.

A weak aroma lingered in the air before disappearing. Tante Gisela didn't have sugar, so cookies didn't smell or taste the same. Tante Gisela had told Ilse all about rations a few months ago.

"The Germans are cutting our food supply and redistributing it for the German population. So, we have to make do with less food. I don't know how much longer the inn can hold onto business either," she had said.

Things were changing very quickly. It had only been several months since summer, when everything was good.

"I had a farmer friend who brought me food in secret until November, but ever since it's been a lot stricter. I had to borrow flour from the employees,"

Tante Gisela said, burying her head in her hands. "I don't know how on earth I'm going to make a Christmas dinner."

"Don't worry, Tante Gisela," Ilse had told her. "We'll find food. There's only two of us, after all."

Really, there was three. Ilse still brought food to Leon every day, though the amount he desired increased weekly. Ilse was eating less so she could bring him more to eat from her portion. Ilse didn't really mind, since it was nice to have a friend to talk to.

Tante Gisela combed through the box, and she picked up a photograph. She threw it down, immediately, and her lips tightened. Her eyes grew wider, and she climbed back down the ladder. Her eyebrows furrowed. Ilse could tell that her mood shifted.

The radio was still blaring some news from Vienna when Tante Gisela stalked across the room and shut off the radio.

Tante Gisela put on a fake smile.

"Oh, I'm sorry Ilse. You know…I'm just frustrated with erm…" Tante Gisela paused to think for a moment. "Th…the news story. Yeah. Ruhm being commissioned to write a book on wartime cooking… Ridiculous right?"

Franz Ruhm was a Viennese chef and radio broadcaster. *What's so frustrating about that?* Ilse wondered.

Autnt Gisela sighed, folding the ladder. "I think I'm done decorating for the night. I'm a bit tired. Can you take the cookies out of the oven and put yourself to sleep?" She lost the fake smile.

"Of course, Tante Gisela."

She nodded, pulling on her sweater. "Goodnight, Ilse."

"Goodnight," Ilse said, watching her trek up the stairs. Her door closed and Ilse heard a soft creak from the bed.

Ilse grabbed an oven mitt from the basket on the counter and pulled the cookies out. They looked funny and didn't smell sweet.

Ilse counted the cookies on the large pan. There were fifteen. *I'm sure Tante Gisela won't notice if I take some,* Ilse thought. She carefully pried two off the pan and wrapped them in a cloth napkin.

Ilse glanced outside. Spiky bits of ice hung off the window like glassy fingers, and Ilse shuddered glancing at it. She wrapped herself in Tante Gisela's coat and stole two blankets from the cabinet near the bookcase. Ilse wondered how Leon was managing tonight. She could check on him now, while Tante Gisela was asleep.

Ilse crept over to the blanket cupboard where Tante Gisela kept her spare blankets to snuggle in by the fireplace. Ilse looked inside and spotted a heap of fuzzy blankets inside. Leon certainly needed them more than her. She stuck her arms into the cupboard and started pulling. She was frozen, trying to grab onto the pile of blankets, and her arms got stuck in the pile. Ilse didn't move for a few seconds, until she gave her arms a yank and she came tumbling away from the cupboard, a stack of nearly ten multicolored blankets following her.

Ilse pulled on her boots and tucked her pajama pants inside them. She hauled the set of blankets into her arms and delicately placed the cookies into her pocket.

Ilse pried the door open, and slowly pushed it shut. The snow wasn't blowing too hard, but the ground was covered in it. You could see Ilse's footprints in the snow as she shuffled up the hill.

When Ilse entered the barn, she could see that Leon was sleeping. He had used the horse saddle as a pillow.

The gust of cold air woke Leon up, and his eyes watered at the sight of the outside. He yawned, stretching his arms upward. His slightly chubby cheeks were slimming down.

"Ilse, what are you carrying?" Leon asked.

Ilse threw the stack of blankets onto the ground. "I have warmth! And a little treat," she said. Ilse knelt down, unwrapping the napkin. She held the cookie up to him.

Leon's eyes widened. "Is that a real cookie?"

Ilse giggled. "No. There's no sugar, so it's a bit dry, but I thought you might like to have it."

When Ilse came much closer to him, she could smell the stench of hay, sweat and dirt caked into his pajamas. She put her hand to his shoulder.

"I'll bring back some real food tomorrow, okay? You know, Christmas is coming around the corner, and Tante Gisela is going to make a feast. We'll have bread dumplings, sauerkraut and chocolate cake," Ilse said.

Ilse knew she lied again. Deep down, she also hoped that there would be a lot of food to eat. Again, what Leon needed was hope, so Ilse figured she'd give it to him.

Leon nibbled off the rest of his cookie and leaned his head against the wall. "Ilse, can you bring me new clothes? I'm tired of these and I haven't bathed at all for a very long time."

Ilse noticed Leon's pants had grown shorter, and his calves were exposed. The pajama shirt smelled mildewy and grew shorter on him.

A lightbulb went off in Ilse's head. "Leon, it's snowing."

He shrugged. "As it does in Austria."

Ilse rolled her eyes. "Go outside and rub some snow over all the dirt on your body! It can get rid of it for the time being, and I'll bring soap every time I visit."

Ilse gasped. "Tante Gisela hardly spends any time at home, Leon. You can come through the side door during the day and bathe."

Leon rolled his eyes back at Ilse. "It's also very, very cold, no?" He motioned to Ilse's jacket.

"Five minutes is all it takes."

Leon giggled. "Alright, Mother Ilse," he teased.

Moments later, he went outside. It was quite dark, so Ilse couldn't see him but she could tell he was grabbing heaps of soft, powder-like snow and rubbing it over his body. Ilse heard some laughs of excitement, then she saw Leon quickly hurry back inside.

Leon dried off with a spare blanket, which he threw up on a rafter to dry off.

"Goodnight, Ilse." Leon hugged Ilse and walked her out to the door. "Thanks for everything. I'm going to completely cover myself in these blankets."

Ilse smiled. "Of course. I'll come back soon," Ilse said.

Upon Ilse's return to the house, her memory was jogged when she looked at the pile of unhung ornaments and radio. *Surely* a cookbook didn't set off Tante Gisela.

Ilse walked over to the box on top of the ladder. The cardboard was weak and bendy, so it was easy to pry the lid off. This particular box of ornaments had photographs embedded in the design of the ornament.

A photograph of a young, glee-filled boy in overalls filled the center of the photo. Tante Gisela was on the right, with a large, joyful smile. Her arm was wrapped around the boy. Ilse flipped the photo to see the description.

Otto Kofler, 1932. Age 4.

Tante Gisela's son stuck with Ilse throughout the month. She looked so young in that photograph that it must've been *ages* ago that her son passed. Ilse didn't think too much of what Frau Kofler said about Tante Gisela's son, but now Ilse know the memories came back and affected Tante Giselar a lot more than how Ilse thought it did.

I mean, if she had the photograph of him, she must have some of his belongings, right? I did have an idea of where she put his things, Ilse thought.

Ilse hadn't quite ventured around past her room, which at the top of the stairs. The washroom was directly across from her bedroom, so she didn't exactly have a reason to go down the hall. Though, when passing by the hall, Ilse *did* always see a small square door in the ceiling. That door posed a mystery she couldn't answer.

Ilse saw the dark, lonely attic door at the end of the hallway whenever she came up, but something about its detachedness from the rest of the house scared her away from it.

Then of course, Ilse knew she had to find Leon clothes. Ilse had brought him some thick woolen sweaters she found in the back of Tante Gisela's closet, and he was doing fine in those.

Ilse also thought a lot about her parents. She wondered if they were shopping for gifts right now, drinking hot cider and reading books. Eventually, Ilse decided that they *must* be getting a new apartment. After all, Ilse would need a welcome surprise, right? *They are probably waiting for me right now,* Ilse thought.

But that couldn't be true. *If I have to hide, they must have to hide too,* Ilse thought.

But no. *They were arrested, right?* Ilse questioned.

Everything was blurring. Ilse pushed the thoughts away.

Christmas was fast approaching, and Tante Gisela had scrapped bits of rations here and there to save for a Christmas dinner. She said she was making a surprise, so she didn't tell Ilse the details about the dinner. Ilse just knew it was going to be good.

The fire spit and crackled as Ilse fed it bits of wood from the pile by the fireplace. A fair of smells came from the kitchen: earthy greens, and some unidentified scent. Ilse turned her head playfully.

"Ilse! Back around," Tante Gisela called to her. She attempted to cover the counter with her arms.

Ilse laughed, turning to face the fire. "Whatever secret meal it is, you can show me."

"I would never," Tante Gisela replied.

Thoughts of the attic barged into Ilse's head. "Tante Gisela, I'm going to head upstairs."

"Alright!"

Ilse figured Tante Gisela wasn't really listening to what she was saying, which gave her the perfect opportunity to explore the attic.

Ilse ran up the stairs, taking them two at a time. It wasn't easy in a robe, but she managed. At the top, Ilse walked past the line of sight from the kitchen, and Tante Gisela didn't question it. She was too immersed in cooking.

Ilse tread lightly once she got farther down the hallway. *What is in that attic?* Ilse wondered.

The door stood like a giant above Ilse. She ran to grab a chair out of Tante Gisela's room, and then she climbed up and touched her finger to the door. Ilse pushed it door upward, and a coat of dust came off, onto Ilse's face. She could see her handprint on the door. Ilse jumped upwards from the chair, landing inside the attic with a thud.

A rush of dust blew in Ilse's face and mouth, which was coincidentally wide open. Ilse had never regretted it more. Boxes upon *boxes* upon *boxes* were all that filled the room. Ilse stepped in, waving her hand over the dust in her face. Ilse leaned in to read the label on one of the boxes.

Otto's Clothes, 5. Was it merely a coincidence that the first box I looked at belonged to her son? Oh, and five boxes of clothes? That's way more than I had in Vienna, Ilse thought. She looked around. The attic was bigger than her old bedroom.

Ilse hauled a cardboard box off the top and dropped it on the ground. A singular piece of tape closed off the top, so Ilse used her fingers to bore through it. Tante Gisela clearly never came in here, and if Otto had several boxes of clothes, what harm would it be to take some for Leon?

The first thing in the box was a pair of red, plaid pajamas. Ilse held it up. They looked to be about the size for a seven- to eight-year-old boy. She would *definitely* be taking those. Next, was a woolen cap. Ilse went through, picking out winter wear to help Leon withstand the temperatures for now. She was sure that *some* of the boxes in the room contained summer clothes. Ilse figured she could come back later to get it.

Ilse hid the clothes into the back corner of her room. She beamed. Leon would be pleased.

Ilse had one last day of school before Christmas Eve. There weren't as many talks of war, or progress from any fronts, so Ilse tried to tuck it away in her mind. Tante Gisela's grand meal for two was still in the works, and Ilse was excited for the reveal when she returned from the inn later today.

Fraulein Ingrid decided that the class would visit the church again. The class hovered at the front of the towering building like they had many months ago during the first visit. The air was still, but the temperature sent chills up the children's spines. Greta shivered and scooted closer to Ilse.

The church bell tolled, and the squeaky wooden door slid open. The group filed into the pew at the back of the room next to the confessional, and everyone started praying.

Sitting in the cool, practically empty church Ilse couldn't help but think about Leon. How was he doing, being cooped up in a barn for a whole month? He didn't even go outside. If Ilse was shivering after being outside for only a few minutes, how could she expect Leon to be well? Ilse knew she had to get him help.

She had to think. Fast.

The evening was exactly what Ilse expected it to be. The room was illuminated with Christmas lights and candles, and the aroma of vanilla spread through the open floor. The fireplace crackled and provided a comforting and beckoning sense of safety. Snow lay thick across Maria Alm, and Ilse had never felt more grateful to be where she was.

Dinner was cozy– just enough for two, maybe three people. For obvious reasons, there wasn't a stuffed goose or carp, and vegetables were sparse. Tante Gisela prepared the most delicious and delectable bratwurst with roasted potatoes, which she had gotten from a friend. There was no chocolate cake with cream like Ilse had hoped, though Tante Gisela did bake some more tasteless vanilla crescent cookies. Ilse didn't touch those.

The pair lounged in the living room after dinner. Ilse wrapped a few bratwurst and potatoes and left it on the counter. "I'm saving it for later, in case I get hungry," Ilse said. "Thank you for the amazing year, Tante Gisela."

Ilse smiled. *Where would I be right now without her?* Ilse thought.

Tante Gisela's eyes sparkled, and Ilse sensed a bit of longing in her heart. *Was she thinking about Otto?* Ilse wondered. She hugged her.

"Goodnight," Ilse said, standing up.

"Wait." Tante Gisela's warm tone stopped Ilse, and she sat back down. Tante Gisela smiled warmly. "Wait here. I have a surprise for you," she said.

Tante Gisela tiptoed to the Christmas tree, and slipped out a small, rectangular package. It was wrapped in old newspapers, and Ilse could tell it was a book. She didn't even notice the package was under there. Ilse didn't get Tante Gisela a gift, so she certainly didn't expect one from her.

Regardless, Ilse was excited. It'd been so long since she received a gift!

Ilse ripped off the paper, and out came a beautiful, hardback copy of a picture book. The title *Madeline* ran across the top, and a picture of the Eiffel Tower and little girls dressed in yellow were painted below. Ilse opened the book to the first page, and read aloud:

> *"In an old house in Paris*
> *That was covered in vines*
> *Lived twelve little girls*
> *In two straight lines."*

Ilse looked to Tante Gisela, and threw her arms around her. "Thank you." Ilse said.

Tante Gisela smiled. "It was nothing at all. I'll be heading to sleep now, we have to wait for St. Nikolaus to arrive, right?"

Ilse chuckled and waved to Tante Gisela as she ascended the stairs.

The moment Ilse's skin hit the air outside, she felt alive and free. The food for Leon wouldn't stay warm much longer, so she had to hurry. Ilse rushed up the hill, and to the barn. She rapped on the doors, and Leon's smiling face greeted her.

"Ilse! I've been waiting for you all day," Leon said.

Ilse laughed, hugging him. "I've brought you a present," Ilse said.

Leon looked confused. "A present?"

Ilse presented the plate of bratwurst and potatoes. Leon's eyes lit up like Ilse had never seen, and he took the plate, gobbling it up. He lay against the wall, rubbing his tummy.

"That was the best meal I've had in a long time. And the most I've had to do in a long time," Leon said. He beamed.

"Leon, I have one more thing that St. Nikolaus left for you," Ilse said.

Leon giggled. "I don't think St. Nikolaus is real. He never visited or left me gifts," he complained.

Ilse shook her head. "He must've made a mistake because I've got these for you." Ilse grabbed the pile of clothes hid in her coat and presented them to Leon.

His eyes watered. "Are these clothes for me?" He squealed, holding up the shirts and pants to his body, trying to get a sense of the size. Suddenly, he dropped them. Leon jumped into Ilse's arms and hugged her tightly. "Thank you, Ilse," Leon said, muffled by Ilse's shoulder.

Ilse laughed. "It's the least I could do," she said to Leon.

After a while, the clothes were folded and tucked into a corner. Ilse wrapped Leon in layers of the spare blankets from many months ago. He giggled as Ilse spun him like a spider in a cobweb.

"I'm going to get going, alright?" Ilse said.

Leon playfully pouted, but quickly smiled. "Merry Christmas, Ilse."

Frostbite

January 1940, Maria Alm, Austria

At the beginning of 1940, Tante Gisela decided to enroll Ilse in Sunday school classes. "They will help you pass your Confirmation," she had said. Ilse didn't even know what a Confirmation was.

Fraulein Ingrid passed out a book to each of the students, similar to the one that Frau Kofler gave Ilse. They all had illustrations of Jesus on the cover, with lots of nature and animals all around him.

"Class, these will be your textbooks for the next few months," Fraulein Ingrid said in her shrill voice. "I expect you all to read the stories and be able to tell me details about them."

Ilse glanced over at Georg, who was already skimming through the book. Greta was reading the back cover. Ilse didn't want to read the book. After all, she wasn't Catholic. Ilse figured she shouldn't have to read it or memorize the stories. Ilse crossed her arms and stared at the floor.

"Ilse, open your book," Fraulein Ingrid said from the front of the classroom. Ilse gave her a side-eye, and then flipped her book to a random page.

That just doesn't feel right to me at all, Ilse thought. She didn't want to take Sunday school classes. That wasn't who she was. *What would Father say about me being here?* Ilse thought.

When Ilse did think about it, she figured that Father might say it didn't mean anything, that it was just a class, and she had to do it to live. He would say that she had to put on a show. Ilse just didn't like being put in a box where she had to conform to being a certain religion.

Ilse leaned over her book, starting to read. Only because Father would've wanted her to.

Greta told Ilse about it later. "It basically initiates you into the Catholic faith," she had said. "You'll pick a saint name to be your Confirmation name, and then there is supposed to be a person to bless you in. I don't remember the details," Greta said, staring at the sky. "You don't know what it is? You hadn't heard about it at all in Vienna?"

"Oh, my family just didn't think that far ahead," Ilse said.

The wind was cool, and Ilse's teeth were chattering. Snow was piling onto rooftops. Ilse's fingers would've frozen right off if she took them out of her double-layered gloves.

"Forget it," Ilse said. "I can figure it out later," she trailed off.

Greta nodded. "You've always been a hard worker. I'm sure you'll be fine, especially now that we're going to a new teacher."

Ilse sighed, but smiled. "The time is passing by so fast. I can't wait to be done with primary school," she said.

Greta shrugged. "I already know what I'm going to do once I finish school," she said.

Ilse raised her eyebrows. She had no plans or ideas for what she was to do with her life. *Maybe I'd travel, or be an astronomer. Were Jews allowed to be astronomers?* Ilse wondered.

Greta sat down on the bench by the fountain in the square, and she crossed her legs.

"I'm going to move to America," Greta said after a few moments of silence.

Ilse widened her eyes. "What part?"

Greta thought for a moment. "I'm not sure. I'd like to be a movie star, or something. Maybe a big city."

Ilse turned to her, smiling. "Can I come?"

Greta laughed. "Of course. We can live together," she said. "And what will your job be?"

"I'm not sure. I think I'd like to go to university and be an astronomer," Ilse said.

"I didn't know you were interested in astronomy."

"It's nothing terribly serious. My father and I used to read about stars and stories about constellations, but I just thought it would be nice."

"No. That sounds absolutely amazing, Ilse. You should do it. Once we get out of here." Greta opened her arms to the sky. "Find out what's all the way up there."

Ilse laughed. "I go stargazing at night sometimes. You should come with me," Ilse said. "But I really like it here. In Austria. I don't think America has the same kind of stars."

Greta tilted her head around the square. "I suppose. But I need an adventure, you know?"

"I've never actually left Vienna ever since I was born, so Maria Alm is an adventure for me every day," Ilse said.

"Your life is so interesting, Ilse. You could write a book about it, you know."

Ilse chuckled. "I've stopped reading a lot recently. I think I'd better get into the swing of it again if I'm to be an author."

Greta stood up stretching her legs. Ilse noticed that Greta didn't seem any taller than she was when she first met her.

"An astronomer, writer and movie star. We'll be unstoppable," Greta said.

"In America, too," Ilse added.

"I'm glad to have you, Ilse."

"I'm glad to have you too, Greta."

"Listen, I'd better get going. Mother might expect me back by now," Greta said.

"Go home. I have to go to the inn to get something anyways," Ilse said.

Greta leaned in and gave Ilse a big hug.

"Goodbye, Ilse, I'll see you tomorrow!" Greta called as she turned the corner around the inn and disappeared.

After Ilse had gotten a plate of food from the cafe, she traipsed up the hill and towards the barn. Ilse was careful not to drop anything or slip on the snow.

The barn looked sad. The red paint chipped and grew more faded each day Ilse came. Ilse left Leon books from Tante Gisela's library to entertain himself with. Over the past month, with Ilse's help, Leon had begun to learn letter names and simple words. There was of course, much left to be done.

Ilse knocked on the door and heard a hacking-cough come from behind.

"Leon?" Ilse called out. She heard coughing in response.

Ilse pushed the door, which came open to her surprise. Ilse immediately spotted little Leon crouched in the corner, coughing away.

Ilse nearly dropped the plate of food rushing over to him. She slid it to the corner and heard a thud as it hit the wall. Ilse rushed to Leon and he sneezed loudly.

"Leon, what's the matter?" Ilse asked.

Sweat started to pool at the back of Ilse's neck, and the hairs on her arm stood up. *I failed. I failed to find him a safe place and instead, I left him in the barn to get sick.* Ilse had a myriad of thoughts running through her head.

Leon spoke in a low, tacky voice, which completely contrasted his usual, high-pitched tone. *I'd only been gone for a day. What could've possibly happened?* Ilse thought.

"Ilse," Leon said. "I don't feel good."

Leon burst into tears. "My skin is prickling and my fingers are white."

Ilse glanced down. They were paper-white and thin to the bone.

Ilse's heart started racing. "Leon, we're going to get you some help," Ilse said.

Ilse grabbed all the blankets she could see, and cocooned Leon in layers of thin wool. He looked to be plenty warm after about four blankets, so she stopped. Ilse darted her eyes around the barn. *How could I get him down the hill? I knew where I had to go, but how could I get there?* Ilse thought.

A round, disk-like wooden slab leaned against the piles of farm tools. It had the width of both of Ilse's arms, and it was smooth on one end. It must've been scrap wood when they were building the barn. It would make do.

Ilse coaxed Leon out of the barn, and his teeth chattered when a breeze came by.

"Leon, sit on the wood," Ilse said in a sweet voice.

Leon huddled himself in the center, and breathed into his hands to make heat. The sun would be going down quite soon. Orange and yellow hues were drowning out the open blue sky.

"Hold on to the edge," Ilse said. Leon took out one hand from his blanket, with what Ilse thought he would hold on with, but he covered his watery sneeze. He grabbed onto the edge.

"Okay, Leon. Hold on tight, I'm pushing you down the hill," Ilse said. She heard a groggy, indistinguishable reply.

With both arms, Ilse pushed the saucer over and down the slope. It shot down way faster than she thought it would, similar to how a bug would shoot up from your leg after you caught it giving you a bite. Ilse ran down the hill, trailing just behind the wood that slowed to a halt once the ground flattened.

Ilse silently prayed that no one would be on the road, and she sprinted to the side door as fast as you could holding a seven-year-old boy.

Ilse set Leon down, putting her arms around him.

"You're going to be okay," Ilse whispered to him.

Ilse opened the door and carried him to the couch. She dashed to the sink, trying to churn out a cup of hot water. Ilse heard footsteps behind her.

A very confused Tante Gisela was descending the stairs, and her eyes widened at the sight of Leon on the couch.

"I need help," Ilse said breathlessly. Tante Gisela promptly dashed down, and Ilse made her way to a very drowsy Leon. She pressed the cup against his hands and face.

"Tante Gisela," Ilse said. "This is Leon."

"Leon, are you okay?" Tante Gisela said. Her normal, calm voice was now concerned and slightly frantic. "Ilse, who are his parents? I can send a message through, or go to their house–"

"Stop."

"What? Ilse?"

"Leon doesn't live here. Leon is in hiding in the barn up the hill." Tears were beginning to pool in Ilse's eyes. "I don't know what to do," Ilse cried.

"His fingers are so cold and he's sneezing and his voice is different, and I…."

Thoughts were stirring in Tante Gisela's brain, but Ilse could tell she was trying to push them away to focus on the moment. Tante Gisela dashed to the kitchen and pulled out a drawer full of washcloths. She removed a few, soaked it in hot water and pressed it to Leon's forehead. Straight after, she dashed to the coat closet and pulled on a large black coat.

"I will go to the village doctor. You decide a cover story. I trust you to do so. Leon will be safe." Tante Gisela leaned in to hug Ilse, and Ilse hugged her back.

Tante Gisela walked out the door, shutting it, and Ilse peered out the window to see her walk down the winding road.

Leon would be fine, the doctor said. A mild case of frostbite and a cold wouldn't take too long to wear off. Just take a bath, he said, at 40 degrees for a week and Leon would be good as new.

"And how did your little friend get frostbite, Ilse?" The doctor asked.

"Erm, he played outside for too long without gloves. Or a jacket. And he kept going out with wet hair in the wind. So he caught a cold," Ilse said.

The doctor shook his head, clicking his tongue. "You children are so stubborn these days," he said. "Don't forget to take a bath, and you'll be good as new. Take care," the man said.

The doctor put on his coat and walked out the door. It had begun to snow again.

Once the doctor was far out of range, Ilse turned to Tante Gisela.

"Thank you."

Tante Gisela waved Ilse off. Ilse noticed a difference in Tante Gisela's face. She could tell Tante Gisela felt tense and sullen.

"I'm glad to meet you, Leon," Tante Gisela said. "Leon, have you been staying in the barn up the hill for a while?"

Leon was sipping on a mug of hot water. "Yes. Ilse has been keeping me company and bringing me food."

Tante Gisela turned to Ilse, a frown flickering across her face. "You can call me Tante Gisela."

Leon sneezed, and wiped his nose on his pajamas. *Otto's.*

"Ilse, can I talk to you? Leon, stay on the couch." Tante Gisela beckoned Ilse upstairs.

Once the pair entered to Ilse's room, Tante Gisela closed the door.

Her demeanor shifted immediately. "Ilse, what on *earth* were you thinking?" Tante Gisela said sternly.

"What do you mean?" Ilse was so confused. She thought Tante Gisela would be proud of her for saving Leon.

"Ilse, it's too dangerous to take in another child. Why did you take up this responsibility?" Tante Gisela crossed her arms, and Ilse could see her eyebrows were furrowed.

"I *had* to! Did you want me to let him starve?" Ilse was angry now.

Tante Gisela scoffed. "I'm having enough of a hard time finding the means to support *us*, let alone another person. Think before you act," she said spitefully. Tante Gisela stormed out of the room.

Mother and Father certainly wouldn't act like this. Ilse's body was tingling all over. Maria Alm didn't feel so right anymore.

Why was she acting different all of a sudden? What did I do so wrong? Ilse buried her head in her arms and sobbed.

13

The Plan

January 1940, Maria Alm, Austria

Tante Gisela came up to Ilse's room later that evening.

Knock, knock. "Ilse, are you there?" Tante Gisela asked.

Ilse didn't want to be. Ever since the fight, Ilse had stowed herself away from Tante Gisela. She had spent the last few hours reading a frayed copy of *Moby Dick* that she found on her floor.

"Come in," Ilse said blankly. Ilse knew it wasn't even her space to grant Tante Gisela permission to enter.

Tante Gisela came in and sat down on the edge of the bed. Ilse set down her book and stared at the bedsheets.

"Ilse," Tante Gisela said gently. "I didn't mean to flare up on you like that. I'm so sorry I acted that way."

"But why did you get so mad? I was only trying to help Leon," Ilse asked.

Tante Gisela nodded and sighed, inching closer to Ilse. "It's just a lot of pressure from everything. The inn, the workers, the guests."

"Ah," was all Ilse could reply with.

They sat in silence for a few moments.

"It- It's not exactly true," Tante Gisela said out of a sudden. "Well, it was only partially true. I-, I-, I've been thinking about my son recently. Leon reminds me an awful lot of him."

"I didn't know you had a son," Ilse lied.

"I do– did. He passed away a while ago."

"I'm so sorry."

They locked eyes for a moment, and then Tante Gisela darted her vision away from Ilse.

"It's been hard. Erm, the boy, the boy, Leon–?"

"Yes. Leon."

"Leon reminds me of my son."

I had no idea that Leon reminded Tante Gisela of Otto, Ilse thought. *I didn't want to hurt her.*

And Tante Gisela told a white lie, only because she was hiding the pain of losing her son. Ilse then realized that the reason she was lying was to try and protect herself from her old life, just like Tante Gisela. Ilse had to lie about what she did at night and how she hid Leon. She sheltered that part of herself because she wanted to protect those private things about herself. But getting it out in the open with Tante Gisela seemed to make it better.

Tante Gisela sighed. "Ilse, I am more than able to help support Leon. I'm thankful you knew where to bring him in time of emergency. Thank you for caring for him. Now, when I was sitting in my room, I had a thought. My best friend from secondary school is a boy named Darió Claus. He moved to Switzerland many years ago to a small town. As I remember it, he resides near a monastery that has a boy's home attached to it. I could try and send him a letter about taking in Leon. It would be safer than occupied Austria," she said.

Deep down, Ilse didn't want Leon to go. After all, he was one of the only people who knew that she was Jewish. Leon was a great companion, almost a brother to Ilse. She didn't want to fight with Tante Gisela anymore, though. And Leon *would* be safe.

"That sounds like a perfect idea, Tante Gisela."

She smiled. "I will get right on that then."

Tante Gisela leaned in to kiss Ilse's forehead. "I'm going to go make dinner, maybe think out the details. Alright?"

Ilse nodded, and Tante Gisela left the room.

Ilse lay, staring at the ceiling until she heard some tiny footsteps come from behind the door.

"Ilse?" Leon said.

"Hi Leon," Ilse replied softly.

The door opened slightly, and Leon, bundled in his mass of blankets, slipped inside and closed the door. He was holding a croissant on his plate. He came over to the bed and jumped into the covers.

"Tante Gisela said I could move around. It felt good to stretch a little, anyways." Leon giggled. "Thanks for making me feel better, Ilse."

"Not a problem. For now, you'll stay with me and Tante Gisela. I also brought you a surprise," Ilse said, trying to sound mysterious.

Leon giggled. "Show me Ilse," he said. "I'm dying of boredom up here."

Ilse pulled out *Madeline.*

Nothing registered on his face, and Leon looked confused. "Ilse, I only know some of the letters. What do the words say?"

Ilse hadn't given the fact that he wasn't in school a second thought. *My goodness. How far behind was he in his schooling?* Ilse thought.

"I'll read you the story," Ilse said. "Don't worry. I will teach you to read later on."

Ilse read, past the rhymes and the tigers and funny bits. Leon finished his croissant, and laughed at various parts. He didn't look too happy at the parts about Madeleine living in a little girls' home in Paris.

"Ilse, you said I could stay with you and Tante Gisela for now. What do you mean for now? Are you sending me away?"

Ilse's stomach did a somersault. She knew she had to tell him the news. "Leon, I think I found a place for you to go."

Leon's eyes went big. "Where, Ilse, where?" He sounded excited.

Ilse almost smiled. He *was* little, after all. He didn't think far or deep about what she was saying.

"Tante Gisela knows a place for you. There's a home for little boys like you," Ilse choked out. "And it's supposed to be a lot of fun."

"I'm confused," Leon said. "Will I have to live in Madeleine's house? Do I have to get my appendix removed too?"

Ilse laughed. Of *course*, that's why he looked scared.

"No, you won't. It will be in a cute little town in Switzerland, with other little boys to play with. Doesn't that sound fun?"

Leon shrugged, picking at his nail. "Is Paris in Switzerland?"

Ilse slung her arm around his shoulder.

"No. Paris is in France, which is far, far away from Switzerland. It would be fun to make friends and live somewhere safe, right?"

"Ilse, will you be there?" Leon asked.

"Well, um–" Ilse said.

"Dinner's ready!" Tante Gisela called.

"Let's go down," Leon said. "I'm starving."

Tante Gisela, Leon and Ilse were all chewing in silence until Leon decided to break it.

"Ilse told me you could send me to a little boy's home in Switzerland," Leon said.

Tante Gisela looked at Ilse and chuckled. "I suppose you could put it that way. But it is much more than that. It's in a town in northern Switzerland called St. Gallen."

Leon tilted his head and squinted his eyes. "Would I be able to learn how to read? Ilse taught me some letters and words." He was still talking in his nasally voice, but he sounded much better than before.

"Oh, *yes, yes, yes* you would! You would attend school and have little boys your age to play with. Doesn't that sound alright?" Tante Gisela said in her calming voice.

Leon smiled. "I guess that wouldn't be too bad. But I want my mother," he said definitively.

Tante Gisela smiled. "Leon, right now we can't be sure of where your mother is. But what I can tell you is that this home will be a very nice place to stay."

Leon sat upright. "Ilse, should I go to the home?"

Every part of Ilse's body said no. Her voice, her heart and her arms wanted to keep Leon close to her. He was the closest thing to a brother Ilse had. *But what if he got sick again? What if the Nazis found him?* Ilse thought.

"It's very pretty, and very safe, Leon. You should go there," Ilse choked out.

Leon didn't seem to notice her angst. "I will go to the boy's home."

Tante Gisela rested her hand on Leon's shoulder. "I haven't sent the letter to ask my friend if you can go," she said. "But I am sure there will be a place for you, no matter how long it takes to find it."

Tante Gisela stood up. "I'm going to run a bath for Leon, and I'll make sure it's warm. Ilse, keep Leon company." And just like that, she was in the other room.

Leon inhaled deeply. "Thank you *again* for taking me to get help, Ilse. I felt like I was dying in the cold. I went outside, and I was just sitting under the trees for the day. It was chilly, but I thought I would be fine. I didn't want to get my blankets wet, and I just wanted some fresh air, and I-"

"Shhh," Ilse said. "I'm not angry. I'm happy you're well." Ilse felt like the perfect sister, caring for her younger brother. She was proud to have someone to take care of and help.

"Leon, I wanted to tell you something I've been thinking about for a few days."

This seemed to get his attention off whatever his little beady eyes were thinking about.

"What's you are keeping to yourself?"

"Leon, it's what *are* you keeping to yourself. Repeat it for me, please." Ilse made a mental note that she had to start teaching him more. The months in the barn weren't going to go away in an instant.

"What are you keeping to yourself?" Leon said this with a mischievous flair.

Ilse laughed. "All right. Well, Tante Gisela enrolled me in more Sunday school classes. I'm going to a ceremony to make me officially part of the Catholic Church. I'm a bit nervous, to let go of my old life."

Leon bit the left side of his lip, pulling off the skin. All of a sudden, he spoke with the eloquence of a gentlemen diplomat.

"Ilse, you can change as much as you want on the outside. I don't remember anything from the synagogue, from the rabbi, or anything. And I'm quite sure you don't either. You have to do this to survive. So don't go on feeling guilty of anything because you know it's all for show. It's not true in your heart." He whispered in a low tone, and winked.

Leon put it into mild terms. But he did make Ilse think a little harder. About the fact that being Jewish wasn't a huge part of who she was. But it changed her life completely. Ilse didn't remember anything they did in Hebrew school, or in the synagogue, but she was still Jewish. Figuring out what that meant to me would be tough.

"Leon, when did you get so smart?" Ilse said, playfully.

Leon looked at me with a fairly straight face. "I mean it, Ilse."

Tante Gisela came out of the bathroom. "The tub is all set. Leon, there's new towels under the sink. You can help yourself. Ilse, I assume Leon will stay in the spare room tonight?"

Ilse's heart widened at her generosity. "Thank you, Tante Gisela. I think he will."

Tante Gisela waved Ilse off again. "Leon is welcome to stay here for as long as he would like," she said.

Leon went into the bathroom and closed the door.

"Tante Gisela, thank you. From the bottom of my heart."

"Ilse, stop thanking me. Go relax. Be a child for the night, without the weight of another person's being on your shoulders."

Ilse lay back, more confident and more at peace than she had been in a long time.

"I will."

Thanks to Otto Kofler

March 1940, Maria Alm, Austria

For the months after, Leon stayed at Tante Gisela's. Ilse took some schoolbooks from Fraulein Ingrid's classroom when she brought the class out to play, and they proved to be of some use. Leon was sounding out more words and he could read more of *Madeline*.

Tante Gisela was supposed to be at the inn for the day, so Ilse volunteered to stay with Leon for a couple of hours.

Ilse glanced up, past her book. Leon's hair was growing out, and it was almost past his ears now. His fingernails, being more accustomed to the cleanliness of a home, had cleaned out and were quite short, due to Leon's nail-biting habit. Ilse often found bits of nails scattered on the couch or on the floor.

Leon leaned over the copy of *Madeline*. "Ilse, what does 'half past nine' mean?"

"9:30. Half-way between nine A.M. and ten A.M., or nine P.M. and ten P.M." Ilse smiled to herself. *It's funny how he knew what an appendix was, yet not what half past nine meant,* Ilse thought.

Ilse looked down at her own copy of *The Swiss Family Robinson*. She was lucky enough to know how to read that she took it for granted. Her cheeks flushed.

A knock came at the door, which took Ilse by surprise. She didn't think Tante Gisela would be back quite so fast.

Tante Gisela stepped in, pulling the door closed fast. Ilse could feel the breeze from the cool air from the living room.

"Now, what have we got here?" The words were playful, but she spoke in a calm, deep tone that made Leon immediately straighten in his chair and look up.

"I'm reading!" Leon said with a toothy smile.

Ilse laughed. "We're working on it," she said.

Tante Gisela beamed. "I'm very happy you have returned to your schooling, Leon," she said, walking to the kitchen. She poured a glass of water. "I am afraid I cannot be of any help in this area. I was last in school a *very* long time ago."

Ilse nodded. "Don't worry, Tante Gisela. I'm working with Leon on reading and mathematics almost every day. He'll catch up in no time."

Ilse stood up, wrapping herself in her coat and swirling her scarf around her neck. "I think I'd better go," Ilse said. "I'm meeting Greta at the bookstore cafe."

Tante Gisela nodded. "Go, go. I'll read with Leon."

Ilse nodded. "Thank you."

After bundling up in layers of old clothes, Ilse stepped out the door, and felt the breeze in her face.

"*Auf wiedersehen!*" Ilse called.

Ilse strolled down the path.

It was a typical Sunday afternoon—an old couple sat at the bench by the fountain, a few people were sitting at the pizzeria, and some little children were playing with a ball. Not many people to bother or *be* bothered.

Ilse saw a sliver of Greta's small figure ahead of her, sitting on the steps to the bookstore. Ilse ran up the path from the town center, and Greta spotted her at once. Greta sprung up and ran to meet Ilse. A cozy bookshop lay ahead. The sign read *Berndhartt's Books & Baking. Didn't Frau Kofler mention him before?* Ilse thought.

Ilse laughed when she ran, so she was out of breath by the time she reached Greta. She hugged

Greta, but immediately dropped her hands to her knees and panted.

"That was my first exercise I've had in days," Ilse said.

Greta shook her head in disapproval, but Ilse could tell she was being playful. "Let's head inside," she said, dragging Ilse in. Greta pranced ahead, grabbing ahold of the door and yanking it open.

The first thing Ilse saw was the maze of books. Greta took her arm and led her through the hall of books. It smelled like old paper and hot coffee.

Greta and Ilse went through the book maze, and titles started popping out at Ilse like never before. Here's a few she added to her wish list:

The Merry Adventures of Robin Hood by Howard Pyle
The Call of the Wild by Jack London
The Trumpeter of Krakow by Eric P. Kelly

At the back of this wall was a little case of baked bread items. The air was sticky with the scent of yeast.

Now that Ilse thought about it, this reminded her a little of Herr Adler's bread selection. Ilse wondered what had happened to him.

"Two for one! Two for one!" he would call on the street all day long, waving loaves of sourdough. It always worked too. Slews of customers would walk in empty handed, returning to the street with a bag

of two loaves. "Come again next time," Herr Adler would say. And they always did.

Greta walked up to the counter confidently, ringing the notice bell on the desk.

A short, rotund man waddled to the front of the room. He had a full face, unshaven for what appears to have been a really, *really* long time.

"Dory, can we get two hot cocoas?" Greta asked. He gave a single, stiff nod and waddled back behind the door he'd emerged from.

Ilse turned to Greta, confused. "His name is Dory? What kind of name is that?" She'd never heard of it before.

She shrugged. "His real name is Eldora Berndhartt. I've never actually given his name a second thought. But Dory's different. He's always been Dory. When I was little, my mother brought me to this shop for the first time and looked at his name badge, which said Eldora. She didn't think it was a fit name, so we renamed him. That's why I call him Dory. He doesn't utter a word though, so don't try to get a response out of him." She leant against the counter.

Now that Ilse noticed it, she was probably only an inch taller than Dory.

The bakery had the same, dry and flavorless-looking bread treats Ilse saw everywhere in Vienna. She'd never tasted them. Ilse could already tell they would be disgusting. Rationing had gotten the best of Maria Alms' food.

Greta rang the bell, and its little melody was practically nonexistent. Ilse wouldn't have even known she rang the bell if she weren't standing right there. Greta jabbed it frantically a couple of times, but the broken bell persisted.

Dory returned moments later, pushing the steaming cups to us. It didn't smell too good, and it burned Ilse's tongue. The bitter aftertaste made Ilse scowl.

Greta tried to hand Dory the money for the cocoa, but he waved her off and refused to take it. Dory pushed the door open, leaving it swinging behind him as he walked into the back.

Greta put a stack of coins onto the counter, and raised her finger to her mouth playfully.

"How on earth does his business survive if he won't accept payment?" Ilse said to Greta.

Greta shrugged. "He must have his ways."

Greta eased herself onto the couch, and Ilse curled up in the dark blue armchair perpendicular to her. Ilse noticed Greta's hair was messier and had more flyaways hanging around her forehead, but she didn't say anything.

"I haven't studied the science at all," Greta complained. "It's too hard. I don't want to even try to understand. It doesn't matter," she said.

"It was nice to have a break from school, but we have to go back tomorrow. I am sure you will be fine. They cannot kick you out from school," Ilse reassured her. "Especially in *war!*"

Greta giggled. "We used to be quite sick of talking about war, right?"

"Yeah, we did. It's a real thing, though. I'm trying to accept—" Ilse stopped after that. Too many memories, emotions, and thoughts, most of which she did not want to go expose to Greta.

"The Germans captured Belgrade yesterday," Greta said softly. "Father told me he heard it on the radio."

Ilse let out a sigh and buried her face in her hands. Warm tears pooled at her eyes. The nightmare seemed to only continue the way it had for three long years. *How can they gain so much so fast, yet I can lose so much so fast?* Ilse thought.

"I just want to go back to my old life," Ilse said shakily. "I miss my parents so much."

"Shh," Greta whispered to Ilse. "You want to know what the Pope said? He sent out a broadcast that was replayed to my father's radio. 'Let your conscience guide you in dealing justly, humanely and providently with the peoples of occupied territories. Do not impose upon them burdens which you in similar circumstances have felt or would feel to be unjust.' It sounded very serious. I didn't hear the rest of it because the message was stopped and cut off," Greta said.

Ilse's heart grew a little bigger. She smiled, biting her bottom lip.

"I wish everyone thought like that," Ilse said quietly. "I mean I think there's some good in the world. You just have to find it."

Greta placed her hand on Ilse's. "Ilse, it's the human experience."

Ilse tilted her head. "What do you mean?"

"You want to know what my grandmother once told me? 'The human experience is the relationships in which we share happiness, suffering and the search for meaning. You can only determine your own meaning,'" Greta said.

Ilse smiled. "Well, the relationships I share my happiness with are you and Tante Gisela."

Greta nodded. "But what about suffering? Ilse, you are one of the strongest people I know, but even you must suffer in some way."

Ilse took a deep breath in. "In so many ways, I feel like I am betraying my old life by living here. That's something I've been struggling with," Ilse said.

"You can share that with me," Greta said softly.

They locked eyes, and Ilse smiled. Ilse knew that she could share that she was Jewish with Greta, but she wanted to wait for the right time. Ilse didn't know why she had to have it harder than everyone else. But maybe she'd come out a stronger person in the end.

Yip, yip. Scratch, scratch.

"Do you hear that?" Greta said, peering behind Ilse's chair.

"What?" Ilse looked around, trying to listen for the source of the sound.

Yip, yip. Scratch, scratch.

Ilse got out of her chair, and she peered outside the window.

The cutest Tyrolean hound was sitting outside, barking at the window. At *them.*

Ilse squealed. Greta, who had her ear pressed to the floor, jumped up.

"Greta, we've got a dog!"

Greta quickly registered what Ilse was saying, and they pulled their coats on hurriedly. They left their half empty hot chocolates on the counter.

The dog was waiting for them, right where Ilse had seen it. Greta got particularly excited.

"Pretty boy," Greta cooed. "Yes, you are, yes you are!" She was knelt down already, hugging and petting the dog.

Ilse kneeled down. "Hey," she said softly.

The dog's eyes widened, and he tilted his head sideways.

Ilse laughed, petting him.

Greta turned to Ilse. "What are we going to do with him?" Greta asked.

"Well, we've got to take care of him, right? Is it a him?" Ilse asked back.

Greta checked the dog. "It's a he," she said.

"I've never had a pet. I don't know what the first step is," Ilse said reluctantly.

"I'll take him home with me. We have dog food for our Pinscher and I'll tell Mother I had no choice but to bring him with me. But most importantly, we have to name the dog. So think."

And they sat there and thought. For quite a while. Ilse felt her hands freezing and she could see her fingers turn white, so she tried to warm them in her pockets. Ilse still was thinking of names.

"What do you think about Zoomer?" Greta said out of a sudden.

Ilse shook her head. "No."

They sat there for another minute, before Greta spoke again.

"Winnie?"

"He doesn't whine very much."

They sat for another minute, until Ilse spoke.

"What about Otto?"

Greta looked up at Ilse in surprise. "Otto. Cute and short, I like it!" She ruffled Otto's fur.

"Otto, I'm going to take you home with me, alright?"

Otto let out a yelp.

Greta looked to Ilse. "I'll see you tomorrow, Ilse?"

Ilse nodded. "Of course. Forget the science," she added.

Greta gave Ilse a disgusted look. She and Otto walked into town.

Ilse looked up to the sky.

Thanks, Otto.

The next morning at school, all the children arrived much earlier before Greta and Ilse. Ilse saw the four- and five-year-olds, barely up to her waist, meandering around. The middle-aged boys were playing with a ball. The ten- to twelve-year-old girls were huddled in a circle at the end of the field.

Now, Georg, Greta, and Ilse were the oldest in the school. But to be honest, Ilse would rather wander off alone than talk to Georg.

Out of sudden, Georg popped out from the side of the school next to the path.

"Where's Greta?" Ilse asked him.

Georg huffed. "She's coming. She's bringing this *ridiculous* dog she found because our parents can't look after him today." He stormed up the creaky wooden stairs and into the school.

Ilse looked down the path. A breathless Greta was jogging down the path. Her bright red backpack was jumping up and down, and Otto, his leash trailing behind, was in her arms.

Greta set Otto down as soon as she came to the end of the path and dropped her hands to her knees. It was much warmer than it was yesterday, and Ilse could feel spring in the air.

Otto ran to Ilse, and she cuddled and swooned at him for a while, until she noticed the group that had formed behind her.

"Can I touch him?" One of the four-year-olds was hovered over Ilse's shoulder. Ilse glanced around.

Everyone in the schoolyard was directly behind Ilse, trying to catch a glimpse of Otto. Ilse turned around, holding him up.

"Anyone want to pet him?"

A clamor of children rushed at her, and they huddled around Greta and Ilse, trying to learn about the dog.

"Where'd you find him?" one of the kids asked.

"We found him behind Berndhartt's," Greta said.

"What's his name?" they questioned.

"Otto," Ilse replied.

The pandemonium continued for a while, until a tall, stocky character appeared behind the crowd. A boy with nearly black hair, dressed in a red striped shirt and overalls parted the crowd of children. His hair was neat and short, but long enough so that his head didn't look flat. His eyes were dark and mysterious. Ilse thought he was cute.

The boy crouched down, and he smiled. It was the purest smile Ilse had ever seen, not to mention his blue eyes glittered in the sun.

Greta frantically poked Ilse's arm. Ilse gave her a sideways glance, and her face looked like she was holding in a giggle fit.

The boy glanced up. "He's nice," he said to Ilse. "Is this your dog?"

Ilse was grinning ear-to-ear at this point. "He's mine and Greta's," she said smoothly, motioning to Greta.

The boy smelled like fresh mint. The boy looked side to side, leaning in to Ilse. "Is this the whole school?" he whispered.

"Pretty much," Ilse said. "We're the oldest of the bunch. How old are you?"

"I turned fifteen a month ago," he said, a little louder.

By now, Ilse had let go of Otto, and Greta brought him out into the field to play with the other kids. She winked at Ilse and made a kissy face. Ilse ignored her.

"My name is Ilse," Ilse said.

"Ilse, nice to meet you. I'm Anton," he said. Ilse liked how he was quiet and relaxed.

"And what are you doing in Maria Alm?"

"I'm from Salzburg," he said. "I've just moved here."

Ilse nodded. "Same with me, I moved here about a year ago."

Greta was all over it. She bombarded Ilse with questions the entire way home from school.

"Ilse, Ilse," she kept teasing. "You've found true love."

"Oh, shut up, I have not," Ilse replied.

"Did you see the way he looked at you during mathematics? And the way he asked you for help on the reading?" Greta skipped a few steps ahead.

"Greta, the blackboard is in front of me. I sit in the first row. There was nowhere else for him to look," Ilse replied indignantly.

Greta pranced ahead when Ilse caught up to her. "Anton asked you for help on the science assignment, though," she continued.

Ilse scoffed. "Fraulein Josephine is absolutely hopeless at anything science related."

The teacher for the upper grades, ages fourteen and up, was Fraulein Josephine. She could teach mathematics, German, and history, but she could *not* teach science. Ilse, however, educated the class on a couple of stars and their shapes they formed in the sky. Fraulein Josephine sat back and let her speak. Anton did ask Ilse more questions during break though….

"Maybe you've got a point." Ilse said.

Greta squealed, jumping up and down. "*Oh,* you're so lucky Ilse! He's so cute."

Ilse laughed. "Hold your horses. Nobody has ever liked me," Ilse said.

"Just you wait," Greta replied.

The pair parted ways at the town center, and as soon as Greta was out of sight, Ilse went up the hill.

Ilse knocked on the side door, and Leon's face greeted her. He smiled, moving to the side to let her in.

"What have you been up to?" Ilse asked as she slipped her worn shoes off.

Leon motioned to the couch. "I've been sitting. Thinking about everything."

Leon made his way to the couch, slowly. After lowering himself down, he adjusted his shirt. It was tucked into the same black pants he wore every day. Or maybe he just had several of the same pants. Like Old Lady Klara all over again.

"Leon, how was your day?" Ilse said. She jumped back into the couch.

"It's the same as always. Nothing to do," Leon said. "I want you to tell me a story."

"Of course," Ilse said. "Anything."

"Well, I wanted to know more about your life in Vienna," he said with a sparkle in his eye. "You seemed flustered talking about it last time."

Ilse sighed. "Leon, it's complicated," she said firmly. *Would he understand my relationship with my parents?* Ilse wondered.

"You don't think you would feel better getting it all out?" Leon asked.

Well, Ilse figured he had a point. She hadn't shared much with him other than how she got here in the first place.

"Okay. Well, where do I start?" Ilse questioned.

"Tell me about your parents," Leon said.

"My mother is Polish and my father is Austrian. Mother is quite strict, but Father is very playful and fun. We lived in this funny building, with a cranky old lady and a seamstress, and when the war started the seamstress took me in. Now that I think about it, I wonder how she's doing. When I lived in Vienna, we sometimes went to the synagogue. Mostly on the holidays. I never absorbed much of the faith, so to be defined Jewish is confusing for me. It's more like something that represents my family, so I identify as it, but not because it's a huge part of my life. Why is one allowed to exist and why is the other one's life torn apart? Why do people allow this one small thing to be the *only* thing they see?"

Ilse didn't expect to say the last part, but it felt like a weight lifted off her chest as soon as it came out. The questions that she'd never really thought about, but had stirred inside her for years came out at once.

Leon sighed. "Ilse, the world in which we are living cannot be explained. You have to rely on your own courage and wit to get through this. Don't let the small mindedness of others get to you, Ilse," he said.

Ilse nodded. He was right. She had gotten herself by so far.

Leon lay down, stretching his arms up to the ceiling. "Don't you ever think about where your parents are?"

Ilse's eyes were starting to water. She tried to blink them away. "I used to think that they were at home, singing songs and watching films. Waiting for me."

"And who's to say they aren't?" Leon questioned.

Ilse sniffled. "I heard them get taken that night. The night I moved to the seamstress's house. The building was so empty and scary. There was no life. Now I'm scared for what I'll find if I leave Maria Alm," she said.

"You're never going to know unless you take a leap of faith."

Ilse chuckled. "What do you mean?"

"Ilse, we're *both* here on a leap of faith. The cart and farmer that brought me here, your neighbor's kindness. So, who's to say we won't find peace in the end? Hold on to what connects you to your parents. Have faith that everything will work itself out. Don't be scared. I'll be here for you."

Ilse's heart warmed. He was right. She'd been brave before, and she had to keep her courage.

15

Greta

April 1940, Maria Alm, Austria

Later on that month, Ilse was walking home from the inn after dinner. For some reason, she felt the urge to slow down and admire Maria Alm like she hadn't before. The snow was beginning to retire for the spring. Ilse gazed at the white mountaintops over the church. The lights from the homes shone like dots in the distance. The sky was a gray-blue color. Clouds were beginning to move away, but at a slower pace. It was almost like they didn't have a place they had to be. They could just drift however far they wanted. Lights flickered on and off across the mountainside as the small community winded down for the evening. *This* was Ilse's home.

Ilse's attraction to the quiet town sent jabs into her stomach. *This isn't who I am,* Ilse thought. *My name was Ilse Stadler, and I am a city girl. No. My name is Ilse Stadler. Not was. Is.*

But why, Ilse wondered, did she already begin to feel at home here? It'd only been about a year since she'd arrived. She spent her whole life in Vienna. *I shouldn't be adjusting this quickly. I belong in Vienna,* Ilse thought.

Ilse walked to the bench in the town center and plopped down, crossing her legs and swinging them. Maybe this was about Leon. Maybe she wasn't *really* adjusted to Maria Alm. Maybe she was focusing on how beautiful the world around her was like with him.

Wouldn't it be painful for him to leave Maria Alm? The details were popping out at Ilse because she didn't want to lose the essence of it all in her memory.

Ilse went home. Tante Gisela had left a note on the counter:

Working late tonight. Help yourself to anything in the kitchen. I love you, and I'll see you tomorrow.
Tante Gisela

I love you? She loved me? Ilse thought. She'd always been sweet and gentle, sure. She'd been caring and forgiving. But that was because she was hosting Ilse. That was because she practically *had* to host Ilse.

Leon was fast asleep on the couch, so Ilse crept up the stairs one toe at a time.

Ilse went to lay on her bed. It felt quite odd to her. *The only people who can tell me they love me are my parents,* Ilse thought. *I'm betraying them. They are the only ones I should've had this relationship with.*

Ilse closed her eyes. She wanted to knock the jumble of thoughts out of her brain. Just as she was about to doze off, Ilse imagined Tante Gisela saying it in person.

"I love you," Ilse saw Tante Gisela saying. Why could she hear it in her brain? She'd never heard it in person.

In an instant, Ilse's mind went back to that night. The night she lost them.

Mother had outstretched her arms to Ilse, attempting to pull her into a hug. Ilse could see the words Mother's lips were forming, but no sound was coming out.

"I love you." Ilse could *see* her saying it. But why couldn't she hear anything?

Tears started cascading down Ilse's face. They soaked the right side of her pillow. Ilse turned to the left.

"We will always be with you, no matter where we go—" Ilse could see the thin line of Mother's lips moving. What happened to her voice?

Grief struck Ilse like a train. She had forgotten the sound of her mother's voice.

When Ilse awoke the next morning, her stomach rumbled with hunger. She had forgotten to eat last night. She rolled to the side.

7:45.

Ilse's eyes jumped open with realization. She had school in fifteen minutes!

After shoving on long pants and a thick, woolen sweater, Ilse dashed down the stairs. She bundled up in a winter coat, quickly cut a thick slice of bread and hurtled out the door.

The ground was slick with ice, so Ilse cruised down the hill in her thick boots before rushing across the town square and through the building arch. She ran past the fence and down the lane until she could run no more. The school group was just ahead, and Ilse could see everyone heading inside.

Ilse rushed to the back, weaving her way through the group until she spotted a short, curly-brown haired head. Ilse tapped her shoulder.

Greta spun around. "Ilse! I was wondering what happened to you," she said, pulling her into a hug.

Ilse hugged her back. "I have something to show you. Want to come to my house later?"

Her hazel eyes shone. "I was just going to ask you about that–,"

She was cut off by a yell. "Children, into the building!" yelled Fraulein Ingrid.

Greta giggled. "I'll tell you later."

Mathematics, German, and science filled the day. Fraulein Josephine rapped the board with her piece of chalk, and her nails scratched the board every so often, sending a chill up Ilse's spine. She glanced over to Greta. She was scribbling notes into her red notebook.

Ilse's page was empty. She copied what Greta had, changing bits of words and the order of lists in her book.

"I love you."

The same, familiar, yet distant memory echoed in Ilse's brain. Mother's lips were forming words again. Ilse couldn't see the details of her face, but she remembered Father next to her. His hands were on her shoulders, yes, and he looked concerned. His forehead wrinkled, a bead of sweat pooling at the crease of his brow.

Ilse thought hard and long. Was her voice soft, or was it gravelly? Did she show her teeth at all when she spoke, or was she more tight-lipped? Ilse's heart was slowly sinking to the bottom of her stomach. Why did she forget her, and not Father?

"Ilse?" Greta's tiny, meek voice spoke in the silent classroom.

Ilse looked around. The entire class, including Anton, was staring at her. She glanced down.

Tears were pooling at her eyes, smudging the ink on her paper. Ilse broke out into a sob and ran outside.

Ilse sat on the bench outside the school as the cold wind blew against her face. The bench was old; Ilse could see fingernail carvings in the damp wood. A little heart was etched next to a sad face. Ilse squinted.

Suddenly, Greta was in front of her. She tiptoed to the bench, sliding herself next to Ilse. Ilse's heart was still racing, trying to calm down.

I'm so ashamed. I should've paid attention in class. This is what I get for letting my mind trail off, Ilse thought.

Greta put her hand on Ilse's. Greta stared straight ahead. Ilse looked at her, confused. Was she going to say something? Greta inhaled and exhaled slowly.

"This morning I wanted to ask you if you wanted to visit the bakery together," she said, smiling.

A little part of Ilse's heart warmed. "Of course, we can go. What about class–?"

Greta waved Ilse off. "Forget it."

They went around the school building and on the road with the country fence.

Greta tucked her hands into her pockets. "It's much cooler today, isn't it?"

Ilse shrugged, feeling a little glum. "In Vienna, every street is full of people coming in and out of stores and they when they breathe, you can see their breath in the air. When my mother and I pushed our way through crowds it always felt quite warm in the winter." Ilse held her hands up to the sky. "*This* is freezing. I expected it to be warmer in April."

Greta laughed. "That's just the country life, Ilse. I wish I lived in a city. I mean, isn't it so fun to walk around and go places? Here we have cows and grass."

Ilse giggled. "In Vienna, we have streetcars and,"–she hesitated before adding–"rioters."

Greta upturned her eyebrow. "What do you mean?"

The pair went down the lane with the two big buildings and entered the town square. The sky was still bright blue. A little boy was drawing figures in the snow pile by the inn.

"That's why I came here. You know, the city being destroyed?"

Greta looked confused. "What on earth on you talking about? You came here almost a year ago and I haven't heard anything about this?"

Ilse did a tad of mental math. "Ten months," she said.

They went into the bookstore.

"Dory, can we get two hot cocoas?" Greta asked. He gave a single, stiff nod and went back behind the door he'd emerged from.

Dory came back, holding two steaming cups. Greta pulled some coins out to pay, but he waved them off, going back behind the door. Greta left the coins on the counter.

"Now, I want you to continue what you were saying. About the city." Greta and Ilse walked through another bookshelf maze, plopping down into a cozy armchair.

"Go on," Greta said, widening her eyes playfully.

"Well, Hitler's troops came in the city. My parents decided I should stay with Tante Gisela for a while," Ilse said.

Greta let out her puppy eyes. "Oh my goodness. Not Hitler again, I *hate* that word. It's all anyone has talked about for the past two years."

Ilse's jaw dropped slightly. "I got more than enough *H-word* talk in Vienna," she said. "My mother was driving me insane and she talked up the whole town with 'What about…?' Or 'The Germans did this…' and I wanted to explode!"

Greta nodded. "That's exactly what I'm saying! All Georg can do is regurgitate what Father says."

Greta tilted her head to the side, thinking hard. "Why did that mean you had to move though? Why didn't your mother and father come with you?"

Ilse sighed. Tante Gisela might get mad if she told Greta the truth. But Ilse knew, at her core, that she trusted Greta. Greta would never betray her. Ilse was grateful for the past year of friendship that they'd had, and in the end it meant a lot to her.

Ilse leant in, whispering to Greta. "I want to tell you something. You need to keep it to yourself."

Greta leaned in, drawing her fingers over her lips. "I promise, I will." She looked doubly as curious than before.

"I'm Jewish."

Greta looked a mixture of confusion and scared. Her jaw dropped, and she walked around the table, immediately wrapping her arms around Ilse. "I'm so sorry about every stupid idea in the world against you."

"I will not say anything to anyone," Greta said. "Fraulein Gisela isn't Jewish though. So, your mother became a Jew after leaving Maria Alm?"

"Not even close. Fraulein Gisela's sister is my neighbor. My parents were taken by the"— Ilse paused, quieting her voice—"*Nazis*."

Greta's eyes widened. "Ilse, why didn't you tell me this before?"

"I was just scared you wouldn't want to be my friend. I was told not to tell anyone."

Greta laughed, hugging Ilse again. "Don't be dumb. You know I'll always be here for you, right?"

Ilse smiled. "Yes, yes I do."

Ilse walked home, fast, waving at Greta. Her cheeks were flushed and rosy as Ilse told her the details of her escape into Maria Alm. She'd seen Greta's exact reactions one time before with Leon. Bundled in her winter coat, Greta's eyes would flash with wonder and excitement, yet she still remained sheltered and safe. She didn't have anything to worry about.

But Greta still understood Ilse in a way that could not be paralleled.

Ilse was glad that Greta truly cared about her. In Vienna, school friends Ilse got close with were few and far between. She just went to school and came straight home, hooked onto Mother's arm. Mother's voice hadn't returned yet, but Ilse could hear her father's laughs and sighs at times.

Snow was beginning to come down. So much for winter going away. Ilse glanced at the sky. It was maybe five at the latest.

Ilse had been thinking a lot about what Greta said when trying to find meaning. After everything she'd been through, Ilse knew she had to discern what she valued and what she wanted. *What could I hold onto to get me through the war?* Ilse wondered.

Ilse rolled her neck side to side. She didn't know why the nervousness in her stomach built up so fast. After all, it wasn't like *Ilse* was the one moving. Why did she feel nervous?

Ilse thought about it on her walk up the hill. She had Tante Gisela. She had Greta.

But what would she do without the boy in the barn?

Ilse opened the door. Leon was curled in the corner. He was covered in five layers of blankets and clothes. Otto's. A bit of warmth brewed in Ilse's heart. It was nice to see his things go to good use.

Ilse wondered if Tante Gisela recognized any of the clothes that Leon wore.

"Leon, Leon," Ilse called softly.

He stirred, yawning slowly and sitting up.

"Ilse, I was waiting for you," Leon said, grabbing her around the neck and hugging her. Ilse giggled, realizing what she had been missing all along.

Maybe she found meaning in the relationships around her.

Ilse hugged Leon, feeling even more grateful than ever that she had him.

16

The Department Store

September 1930, Vienna, Austria

The summer after Ilse's fourth birthday, Mother brought her to the department store on Fleichsmanngasse. She held Ilse's hand, leading her wobbling legs down the smooth marble floor. Ilse remembered them stopping in front of the children's aisle. This was one of Ilse's first memories.

Mother's voice hadn't returned to Ilse, but she knew everything she said. Ilse saw the words coming. She *knew* Mother. But she couldn't place a voice to the face.

Why did she miss her more than she remembered her?

Mother wore her best red pillbox hat and her smartest blazer. Ilse remembered Mother's skirt went down to her knees. Ilse tugged it with her little fist when she toddled down the rows. The polka dotted shirt she wore had ruffles that Ilse liked to twist with her hands on the few occasions Mother picked her up.

Mother's face looked so long and elegant, and she maintained the same, raised eyebrow and tight-lipped expression she would keep for the years to come. Ilse turned to look behind them. A little boy and his mother got in line behind Mother. The boy's mother was short and stout, dressed in dull colors. Ilse turned her head proudly. *Not mine*, she thought.

A skinny man in a suit sat at a desk brimmed to the top on both ends with receipts and checks. The salesman didn't seem to be stalled in his typing. Even at the sight of a customer. Mother rapped her nails on the counter.

The salesman tilted his head downwards, and raised his eyebrow, opening his right eye. "A moment, *miss*." He said the last word with a sneer.

Mother bent her arm against the counter. "I want the finest school clothes and accessories for a little girl." She adjusted her hat.

The salesman typed and typed. What could a salesman possibly be writing? A book? He even stopped, opened one eye wide at Mother, raised his eyebrow and went back to typing.

In one swift motion, Mother was behind the desk and she leaned in to him. She whispered in his ear, her red lips smiling curtly. The salesman turned red and flustered, looking embarrassed.

"Yes, *Frau*. I will show you to our selection of"—he peered over the counter, his beady eyes looking down at Ilse —"little girls accessories."

Mother took Ilse's hand and followed the salesman through the sea of cloth and people.

They came upon a colorful display. Mother grabbed one of the kilts and held it up to a plain blue shirt.

"What material is this?" Mother flipped it back and front, feeling the skirt down to the thread.

The man stood with his arms behind his back, heels together. His glasses were on the lower end of his nose and his right eye fluttered closed at random.

"The finest wool in Italy, *Frau*." His demeanor completely changed by this point. Now, he was respectful and obedient.

Mother took one of the dark green shirts off the rack and held it up to Ilse's little body. The hem went to Ilse's thighs. She placed it back on the rack.

"I'd like three kilts, and an assortment of dark blue and green shirts to a total of five. You do measure for accuracy in sizes, am I right?" She bent down slightly to place her hands on little Ilse's shoulders.

Ilse could tell the man wanted to go mad at Mother, but something held him back. "I don't usually do measurements, but I can make an exception," he said, hesitantly.

Mother smiled. "That's just amazing. Why don't you get your tape measure out? We'll wait here."

The salesman skulked back to his desk.

To Ilse's surprise, Mother picked her up and walked over to a school supplies display. Ilse saw teeny backpacks with patterns of stripes and florals, and large, leather backpacks that looked like something an older girl would wear.

"Ilse, which backpack do you want?" Mother bounced Ilse on her hip and smiled. She brushed one of her curls out of her face.

Ilse had scanned the display. She didn't want a drawing on the backpack. The pattern would be much too busy. Ilse remembered seeing a plain, gray backpack. It had random letters written on it, probably in Finnish or Swedish. She squinted, moving her eyes along the row.

And then Ilse spotted it. The beautiful yellow backpack she'd keep for years to come. It never became too small for Ilse's needs. In the middle was a hand embroidered dandelion, bright and perky. The bright yellow contrasted the main fabric of the bag completely, and the black outline highlighted the dandelion.

Ilse pointed. Mother picked up the backpack from the display and handed it to Ilse.

"You'll use this for school. It's so beautiful," Mother said. She took it from Ilse and examined the design. "Just perfect."

All Ilse did was nod, and Mother put her down.

Part of Ilse liked to wonder why Mother even made a deal out of this shopping trip. For one, Ilse didn't even know what she went shopping for. Ilse, at age four, could only observe what was around her without comprehending anything into detail.

Mother maintained her elegant composure when the salesman came back, and she became the tight lipped, uptight mother once more.

Ilse always wondered what she said to the man behind the counter. She liked to think it was something witty and curt that put him in his place.

That's just who Mother was. Quick to think and quick to act.

Ilse remembered that day forever.

Wishing on Dandelions

April 1940, Zell am See, Austria

Ten years had passed since. Ilse was now fourteen.

That first memory with Mother and the dandelion backpack remained tucked into the depths of Ilse's memory until this spring.

Greta and some of the girls from class invited Ilse to swim at the lake in Zell am See, just about twenty minutes south of Maria Alm. The spring's warmth began to take its toll, and Maria Alm didn't have any lakes. Or pools for that matter.

Greta even came by the inn to pitch the idea to a very hesitant Tante Gisela. *Yes*, there would be a group of girls. *Yes*, they would wear the latest skin protectant formula by Franz Greiter. *Yes*, there was a public bus that could drive them to the lake. Greta came prepared with answers for Tante Gisela's never-ending questions.

When Tante Gisela finally said she would think about it, Greta left to go home, happy she had made a difference.

"Will you get back to me by tomorrow?" Greta had asked Ilse. Ilse told her yes; she'd convince Tante Gisela by then. Tante Gisela and Ilse walked back home, and it was still sunny and bright outside.

Tante Gisela and Ilse sat in the living room looking at the old embers in the fireplace. Their bitter cocoa was lukewarm and the mugs remained full. It was much cooler inside compared to the outdoors. They sat like this for a while, before Tante Gisela spoke up.

"Do you know these girls well?" She spoke suddenly, and Ilse coughed to clear her throat in reply.

"Yes, they are our schoolmates. Greta, and the two new girls in our class, Lottie and Freya."

Fraulein Josephine had called Ilse to the school one day in the middle of the summer. She happened to pass by Greta at the pizzeria and told her to come by as well. There stood two new girls: Charlotte and Freya Schuster from Innsbruck. They went by Lottie and Freya. They were tall, blond and beautiful, and Ilse was taken aback when she saw them.

"I want you girls to be friends," Fraulein Ingrid had said. "Charlotte and Freya are new. This is a very small town, and you two are the only teenage girls here," she said to Greta and Ilse. "Be friends."

And so, they were friends. Greta and Ilse had skimmed the surface with the new girls, learning their interests and what they did for fun. Soon, they'd plunge beneath and become better friends on their lake trip. Quite literally.

Greta figured that if they went in a big group, Tante Gisela would be more lenient. *Who could get lost in a big group? What bad could happen to a big group?* Ilse thought.

Tante Gisela smiled at Ilse when she told her how they met the girls. She leaned back onto the couch and pondered for a moment.

"Alright, you can go. I want you to get out of the town for a little. You girls have thought of every nook and cranny of the outing, and I can't say no, can I? I'll give you a bit of spending money, but I don't have much. You can pack a sandwich to go," she said.

Ilse grinned. She didn't care if she couldn't bring pocket money. Ilse grabbed her around the neck, hugging her hard. "Thank you," Ilse whispered.

Tante Gisela waved her off. "I expect you'll want to tell your friend Greta about this, so I'll leave you to go do that."

Ilse showed up at Greta's door later that day.

"I knew she would say yes," she told Ilse, while she sucked on a lollipop. "I'm so excited!"

Now she showed her excitement. "I'll swing by Lottie and Freya's to let them know. Father found a bus in the newspaper from Zell am See. They make a stop at Maria Alm at nine A.M. tomorrow."

Ilse grinned ear to ear. "Of course. I'll see you then," she said.

Tante Gisela gave Ilse a pretty bag made out of blue denim to bring, just big enough for a towel and her lunch. Ilse wore Tante Gisela's old black-and-white striped swimsuit. It was a little small, but would make do for a day.

The town was quiet in early morning, especially now that it was spring. Movement hardly stirred behind the doors of the town square. The sun dawned crisp and clear against Ilse's skin, and it all felt so rejuvenating. The sun was really the first activity the gravel road caught in the morning. Ilse took in a deep breath, inhaling the scent of fresh grass and mountain air.

The bus stop was down the gravel road connected to the main square, and Ilse's legs were starting to get sore as she walked down. Her calves grew warm and her knees wanted to buckle. After some time, Ilse saw the bus station. Greta and the sisters were already there.

Ilse jogged the rest of her way to the stop. "Good morning, guys," Ilse said breathlessly. They were surrounded by grassy hills on both sides of the road.

Lottie and Freya waved to Ilse, and they all sat at the bench under the covered stop.

After a few minutes, Greta stood up. She adjusted her sunglasses and grinned.

"Girls! I am excited for the fun day ahead of us," Greta said, proudly.

"Go on," Ilse said, knowingly.

"Well, the bus stop is supposed to be on the edge of Zell am See, so we can get off the stop there. Father told me he spotted a grassy patch on the lake with some picnic tables, so we can spend some time there. Afterwards, we can go into the town. Objections?"

Ilse giggled. "None."

The town bus came into sight at the end of the road, and it slowly made its way towards the group. When it came to a stop, the doors opened and Ilse saw the very same grumpy man she had seen a year ago in Salzburg. He had a cigar.

Ilse got up first, and she took a step onto the stairs.

"To Zell am See?" Ilse asked.

The man made no reaction, so Ilse spoke a little louder, almost yelling.

"Is this bus to Zell am See?"

The man grunted and looked at the paper on his lap. "Zell am See," he grumbled out. The rest of the group loaded onto the empty bus.

It was only when the bus began to pull out of Maria Alm that Ilse realized she hadn't left the town since she arrived. The grassy hills that enclosed and protected her opened up, and they were in the Austrian countryside. In a way, she was free.

The drive passed quickly. Greta sat next to Ilse. Greta could sense this was a new experience for Ilse by the way she looked at the fields and the rising sun. Greta put her hand on top of Ilse's and squeezed it. Ilse could do nothing other than smile.

The bus passed the Ritzensee Lake and the one street town of Maishofen, skimming past endless fields and towering mountains.

It wasn't long until the looming blue lay in silence before them, waiting for the girls to touch the surface. The bus pulled through the city, which was light with traffic. The sun was out and bright, and for some reason it seemed much clearer under the open sky, with no mountains covering the little haven Ilse called home.

The bus pulled to a stop. The girls got out and strolled past an empty kosher butcher's store and past a traditional Austrian cafe. Once they reached the lakeside, Ilse heard giggles and shouts from Lottie and Greta. Freya was already running to the small sandy patch past the grass. Ilse spun, holding her arms up in the air. *This* was the freedom she'd been craving for so long.

Were these fleeting moments what life was all about? Ilse thought. The sun, the grass and the sky were so perfect.

The girls swam, basking in the breeze and the warm water of Zell am See. They grew hungry after a couple of hours of swimming. Greta spotted a clock in the window of the cafe, so she checked on it periodically. Freya, it turns out, had brought a picnic basket with extra food, so they ended up having crackers and splitting an apple. Each girl brought their own sandwich, so they ate in silence for a short while after that.

"We can taking the sunset bus back home," Greta said. "It leaves the stop at eight tonight."

Greta's dark green swimsuit contrasted the red checkered blanket from the basket. Lottie and Freya were quiet and didn't make small talk. They were exact opposites of Greta and Ilse. Freya munched on her apple slice and Lottie looked off into the distance.

Greta and Ilse picked an assortment of flowers from the banks of the lake and they brought them back to smell and compare.

Lottie spoke suddenly. "When do you guys think this war's gonna be over?"

Ilse almost made a face she would've made if she was sucking on a lemon.

Freya laughed. It was high pitched and nasally. "As soon as they get the Jews out," she said.

Greta and Ilse almost choked on their sandwiches. Ilse made eye contact, and Greta widened her eyes.

Greta scoffed out loud. "Whatever do you mean?"

Freya smacked her lips together, like she was chewing gum. She looked so proud and arrogant Ilse wanted to shove the apple down her throat. She glanced at Lottie. "Our father said that all the Jews in Austria are gone, and they were taken to camps in Poland where they won't come back."

Ilse spoke up. "I mean, we don't know where they are, right? What if they escape from the camps?" Ilse wanted to scream. *Why did I say that?* Ilse thought.

Lottie shrugged. "There's simply no way that could happen. Soon, we'll get sugar and *real* bread, once this all stops." She pushed herself off the blanket and walked to the waterfront. Freya followed, and Greta motioned for Ilse to come as well.

Ilse changed the topic, and she tried to sound confident. "My father told me that you have to skip a rock for every one of your years," Ilse said. her voice was smooth, and neither Lottie nor Freya showed any indication that they thought something was off.

Greta picked up a smooth, shiny rock from the bank. She skipped it twice.

"And what happens if you don't?"

"He said then you won't grow up, but I don't think that's quite true." Ilse laughed, skimming the ground for the perfect rock. She picked one up and skipped it three times, watching it sink into the bottomless blue.

Lottie and Freya side eyed each other. Ilse could've sworn she saw Lottie roll her eyes, almost like Ilse was acting like a child.

"I think we'd better head back," Lottie said. "We've got assignments to work on."

Lottie and Freya were lying right to Greta and Ilse's faces. There was nothing going on in classes.

"Do you know what bus goes to Maria Alm?" Greta asked hesitantly. Ilse could see a small smile forming at the corners of her mouth, almost as if she were glad they were leaving.

The girls looked at each other. "There will certainly be one at some point," Freya said.

"It was lovely to meet you again, ladies," they chimed in unison. *That* made Ilse want to roll her eyes.

They held the corners of the picnic blanket and folded it, half by half, until it fit into the beautiful picnic basket.

"Goodbye," they yelled, walking through the trees and into the main street. "See you soon," they called.

Greta and Ilse didn't go out with them again.

Greta and Ilse spent a few more hours swimming, but they soon grew tired. The cafe had umbrellas on the deck with lots of shade, so when the waiters weren't looking, they slipped under the cool embrace of its shadow. The streets were lonely, the complete opposite of what Ilse had expected a bigger town to look like. Sure, this wasn't Vienna. But Ilse thought it would be *something* more.

The girls explored the small alleys, the farmer's market stand, the dusty clothing stores, and a few grand residences. The sun was going to sleep soon.

There was a path off the main road, but it wasn't maintained nicely. It was the road not taken by many, and it went through a street and it appeared to open up after a few houses.

Greta and Ilse were just passing by the road, due early to the bus stop. As they walked by, Ilse noticed something at the end of the road. She tugged at Greta's arm.

"Don't you see that?" Ilse pointed down the road. It looked bright, like something was there.

Greta squinted. "I have bad eye sight," she said.

"No, look at that. Why does it look so yellow?" Ilse pointed down the thin gravel road.

Greta looked at Ilse with a funny expression on her face. "Only one way to find out, right?" And then she took off running down the road.

Ilse giggled uncontrollably, and followed her. Ilse was running so fast she couldn't even see what she was running to.

Greta stopped a couple of yards ahead of Ilse, and Ilse slowed down once she saw her. "Why'd you stop?" Ilse yelled out. She caught up to Greta, panting.

Greta's mouth was open, and she pointed. Ilse turned her head.

The open water was ahead of them, and the most ethereal field of dandelions Ilse had ever seen shielded them from the blue. They came just over her toes.

That's when Ilse remembered the day in the department store. The first memories of Mother's affection.

Then, Ilse heard it.

"*I love you.*" Ilse could hear Mother saying it, and the high cadences of her voice ringed in Ilse's ears. Mother's voice was regal and composed, but soft.

"*We will always be with you, no matter where we go…*" Ilse could see the thin line of her lips moving and Ilse could hear the despair she communicated on that night. Her heart filled with content.

Greta sensed something was happening when she saw Ilse's face, but she stayed silent in thought. And Ilse remained forever grateful to her for that.

Ilse leaned down to pluck a dandelion from the field and when she came up, a cool breeze gushed through.

Ilse made her wish and released it into the wind.

18

Bittersweet Goodbyes

May 1940, Maria Alm, Austria

Summer was beginning to hit Maria Alm at the end of May. The village dress shop had some spare flower-patterned linen, so Tante Gisela fashioned a dress that Ilse wore practically every day. The sun blazed down onto Ilse's hair, and trickles of sweat ran down her neck.

It was early Saturday morning. Fraulein Josephine rapped at the board.

"Name the Seven Sacraments."

Nobody moved. Ilse glanced over at Greta, who was picking at her nails. Across from her was Georg, who seemed to be drawing on his textbook. Lottie and Freya were staring off into space. Anton was rummaging through his backpack for who *knows* what.

"Let's see…" Fraulein Josephine said out of a sudden. "Anton."

He jumped up, and clearly didn't know what she said. "Me?"

Fraulein Josephine nodded. "Answer the question."

Ilse was at an angle where Fraulein Josephine could only see the left half of her face, so she tried to catch Anton's eye. His dark eyes caught Ilse's.

Ilse mouthed out the answer.

Anton said it in sync with what Ilse was telling him, and Fraulein Josephine nodded.

Anton winked at Ilse.

"Ilse, what is the parable of the importunate neighbor?" Fraulein Josephine asked.

She caught Ilse off guard, and butterflies were still brewing in her stomach from her interaction with Anton.

"It's…it's…the story of a friend who awakes at midnight to help his neighbor because of his persistent pleas, rather than the fact that they are friends."

"Very good," Fraulein Josephine said, turning back to the board.

Ilse rolled her eyes at Anton playfully, and his eyes glittered.

When Ilse glanced to the side, she found Greta was smirking. Ilse gave her a dirty look. She could tell Greta was holding in laughter.

"Class?"

Everyone's attention suddenly shifted to Fraulein Josephine.

"You all have done such amazing work this semester. You've all learned so much and succeeded in preparing for the sacrament of Confirmation."

Ilse glanced around the room, and everyone seemed happy.

"I'll be seeing every one of you at the ceremony tomorrow. Good luck!"

With that rap, everyone stood and left the classroom.

The twins exited first, followed by Georg. Greta walked to Ilse's left, Anton to her right.

"Fraulein Josephine is delusional," Greta said. "Nobody was paying attention except for like, Ilse."

Anton laughed. "She has good intentions. What saint name have you chosen?"

"Cecilia," Greta said. "My mother also chose Saint Cecilia for her Confirmation."

The week before, Tante Gisela had helped Ilse research saints and pick out a patron saint for Confirmation. Ilse chose Josephine Leroux, a French nun executed during the French Revolution. Ilse had no idea who she was, to be honest. Tante Gisela said that if Ilse wanted to represent courage, Ilse could choose her.

"Saint Josephine," Ilse said.

Anton smiled. "Nice," he said.

Ilse and Anton parted ways at the fountain, and their hands brushed.

"Goodbye," he said.

"Bye," Ilse whispered.

He made his way behind the inn, and took a right.

Greta was spinning in circles after this.

"The only thing keeping me alive is you two," she said.

"We never even go out together," Ilse objected. She realized moments later she sounded overly harsh.

Greta was quiet for a while after that. They walked to the bench by the fountain and sat down. She spoke after a couple of minutes of silence.

"Things have been stressful at home," Greta said. "Father and Mother are always bickering over money and the war, and Georg ends up siding with my father against my mother. He's turning into him."

Ilse's heart sunk. "I'm so sorry," she said quietly.

Greta waved Ilse off. "It's nothing you can control," she said. "I'm just glad I get to be out of the house and hanging out with you. It's much better than being cooped up with them."

It was then that Ilse realized Greta fixated on her and Anton because they were a distraction from her home life.

Greta groaned. "Why are we getting so emotional? This is so stupid," she continued.

"No, it isn't," Ilse argued. "Everything is going to be good. We still have to move to America, right? And write our story."

Greta gave Ilse a little side smile. "Yeah."

"I'll see you tomorrow," Ilse said hesitantly.

Greta giggled. "You know I couldn't miss my own Confirmation." She went serious right after. "Ilse, can you attend Confirmation even though you're not Catholic?"

Ilse been waiting for her to ask this. "I have to pretend. The people in town will suspect something if I don't," she said.

"Do you believe in the things we learned in class?" Greta asked. She wasn't accusing. She seemed quite genuine.

Ilse thought back to her talks with Leon.

"Well, no. I don't remember much, but if being Jewish is what my parents are, it's what I am. It's something left that can bond us together. And that's makes me want to learn more about it. I'm going to try to figure out what it means to me when"—Ilse gesticulated in the air—"*this* is over."

Greta nodded. "You're right. I'm just glad you're safe."

Ilse smiled. "Me too."

The air was warm and sticky, and Ilse could hear birds chirping through the square. This was the type of warm where the trees were dewy and the grass was soft on your toes. Summer was getting off to a pretty good start.

Tante Gisela surprised Ilse that morning with a beautiful baby blue dress. Ilse just assumed she'd be wearing her old flower dress. Leon was reading on the couch while Ilse twirled around in her dress.

Ilse had to tell him why she was dressing up.

"Leon, today I'm going to the church, and I'm a part of a Confirmation ceremony. What do you think about that?"

Again, he displayed the intelligence of an old man. "I'm glad you are finding ways to stay safe. Don't worry about the *meaning* of the ceremony. I need you, after all. You are basically my older sister," he blushed.

"I'm proud to be," Ilse said warmly.

What he said about meaning got Ilse thinking about what Greta said. She didn't find meaning in this ceremony. She found meaning in being a friend, child and sister.

They sat in silence for a little and he bit his lip and nodded. "It is only right. I can't tell you I remember what it means to be Jewish, but it's the belief our parents set for us. We'll always be Jewish."

That was a really nice way to think about it. Being Jewish connected Ilse to her parents.

"I think you're right. I have Jewish heritage, but I don't know what it means to be Jewish. Can I still be Jewish?" Ilse sounded ridiculous to herself.

"Just be who you were *before* everything." Leon said. "I think you've been placing too much importance to something that's just always been you."

Ilse glanced up, and they locked eyes.

"I just have to be myself. I'm still the girl who played at the park with her father, the girl who loved the stars. I'm still the red-haired girl who lives on Zirkusgasse. The war can't take my memories away from me. My courage keeps it," Ilse said.

Ilse smiled at Leon. "I will be. I'll be who I was before everything happened." Ilse glanced at the wall clock.

"Thank you, Leon." He smiled a toothy grin.

"Tante Gisela, I'll see you there?" Ilse said.

Tante Gisela was leaning back on her chair, smiling at the two of them. Ilse had only just realized she heard their entire conversation.

"Ilse, you've found peace." Tante Gisela said.

It wasn't a statement, nor a question. It was the *truth. Did I find myself through struggle?*

"I have," Ilse said, beaming. "I feel at home. I think I've realized that people can have two homes. I can remain loyal to my parents and still love you two. Most importantly, I feel like I can still be happy through my relationships with everyone in Maria Alm. I still know I am Jewish, but I shouldn't worry that I'm betraying my parents by finding new meaning around me."

"I'm glad," said Tante Gisela.

The ceremony was beautiful after all.

Of course, Ilse wasn't Catholic. She knew in her heart that it wasn't what she wanted to do. *I wasn't going to let a war make me change me, right?* Ilse thought. That sounded funny to Ilse when she said it in her head.

When Ilse looked down the pews, all she saw were the people that had changed her.

In Georg, Ilse learned not to lose sight of the truth.

In Lottie and Freya, Ilse learned that she needed to lose friends along the way to find out what she stood for.

In Anton? Ilse wasn't quite sure. He did make her happy when she was around him. *Could that be something?* Ilse wondered.

In Greta, Ilse saw a true friend who supported her through her struggles.

In Tante Gisela, Ilse learned to give herself fully to help others in need.

And in Ilse's heart, she felt each person's impact on her that helped her to shine and grow as a person.

In herself, Ilse saw all the stars she never saw in person; a million times brighter than they would've been had she stayed hidden with fear. She saw her ability to love, care and cherish. These were the most beautiful starry parts of a person you couldn't see; you had to feel them.

It was all a blur, and to be honest Ilse didn't remember much of what was said in the church that morning.

At the end of the ceremony, the children lined against the sidewall of the church for a shot on Greta's father's new camera. After a couple of clicks and flashes, he switched it off and put it in its black case.

"It'll be developed once I go through the full roll," he said.

After the photo, Ilse started to approach Greta, when she was interrupted by Anton.

"Can I show you something?" Anton said. When he walked by, he gently brushed Ilse's elbow. "Come on," he said.

Anton led Ilse past the church group. Ilse craned her neck to look at Greta, who had a small smile on her face. She winked at Ilse.

"Ilse, can I meet you at the fountain when you come back?" Greta called out.

Ilse nodded, then looked back at Anton.

"Where's this place you want to show me?" Ilse asked him.

"It's very nice," Anton said. "You'll see."

They walked into the town square, and up the left path, where Ilse could see her house at the top of hill. They went to the right, walking along the row of houses.

After a few homes, they stopped in front of one. It was identical to the rest of the homes in town, nevertheless it was still beautiful. The home had a balcony, with stairs in the front yard leading up to it.

"I live here," Anton said. He combed his hair back a little.

They walked along the side of the house, and in the back was a beautiful garden. Ilse spotted shades of purple, red and blue all across the garden at first glance.

"What do you think?" Anton said out of a sudden.

"They're so beautiful," Ilse said breathlessly.

"Greta told me you saw some flowers in Zell am See that you liked, so I figured you might want to see my mother's garden," he said.

Out of the corner of her eye, Ilse spotted a budding patch of dandelions.

Greta was alone in the town square when Ilse walked back. Ilse's feet hurt from wearing formal shoes, so she was carrying them, walking barefoot on the hot gravel.

Greta was scratching at her leggings, and when she saw Ilse coming, she didn't move. She didn't call out, yell or giggle. She gave me a small smile when Ilse sat down.

"Greta, are you feeling alright? You've been acting funny," Ilse said.

Greta faked a smile. "Tell me where you went with Anton," she said, ignoring Ilse.

Ilse felt bad for Greta. She must be feeling fairly under the weather, there's absolutely no way she didn't hear her.

"Anton showed me the garden behind his house," Ilse said.

Greta squealed, shaking Ilse with both her hands.

"I *knew* you would go out! I'm so happy for you," she said.

"Thanks," Ilse replied. Calling this "going out" was a stretch.

They sat for a few minutes, neither of them saying anything. Greta had that same sunken look in her face she'd had the entire morning.

"Greta," Ilse said reluctantly. "Please tell me what is going on."

Greta sniffled. More silence followed, and then she looked down the road, and up to the sky.

"We're moving away," Greta said softly. "To Graz."

It almost felt like Ilse's stomach was tying in knots. *What would I do without Greta?* Ilse thought. She was losing Leon too. *Why did I have to lose everything?*

"Greta," Ilse whispered.

Ilse could see teardrops falling down Greta's face.

"My father and Georg are staying here in Maria Alm for now," Greta whispered hoarsely. "Mother and I are moving to Graz first."

"I'm so sorry," Ilse said. "I'm so sorry."

Greta wiped her nose on her dress.

"Don't be sorry. They think it would be a good start for the whole family. Mother wants to be closer to her family, because of well, everything in the world, right?"

"Graz is, it's in—"

"It's on the other side of the country." Greta said, her voice shaking. Mother is packing up our things as we speak. We're leaving early tomorrow morning."

Ilse's heart was pounding. "That fast?"

Greta nodded.

They sat in silence.

"What about America?" Ilse said all of a sudden.

"We can still send letters," Greta said.

The birds and the air and the trees didn't seem all that appealing to Ilse anymore.

"I'm so grateful that I've been able to be your friend," Ilse said. "Thank you for helping me to, *survive*, really."

Greta gave Ilse a half smile. "You can't really get rid of me that easily," she said.

Ilse punched her playfully. "We can make it work. Five more years, then we'll be off to America."

Greta stared at the sky, letting the sun warm her skin. "Yeah."

"I'll give you my new address," Greta said. "You'll have to tell me all about Anton, and we can make plans to meet."

Ilse grinned. "Of course."

"Mother told me we're taking a bus to Salzburg tomorrow, you know. Early in the morning. Can you come to the bus stop at sunrise?"

"Anything, Greta."

The pair hugged, and parted ways in the town center for the last time.

The next morning, Ilse waved Greta off from the bus stop. Her mother hauled on their baggage, while Greta passed up the sacks of clothes. Ilse could tell they weren't very organized. Her mother forgot to zip one bag when she tossed it in.

It then settled into Ilse's mind that her best friend was moving away.

Who knows how long it will be until I see her again? Ilse thought.

After everything was off the ground, her mother walked to the back of the bus and sat by the window.

Greta came up to Ilse. Ilse hugged her tightly.

"I'm going to miss you so much," Ilse said. She was crying.

The girls wrapped their arms around each other, swaying and sobbing.

"You're going to do great," Greta said, her voice wobbly. "Don't worry about me."

"Make sure to write every month," Ilse said.

"Of course, I will," Greta said. Greta sobbed into Ilse's shoulder. "Promise me you won't forget me, Ilse."

Ilse looked down at Greta, tears pooling out of her eyes and down her cheek. "You know I could never."

The driver tooted his horn.

Greta climbed aboard the bus, waving to Ilse. The bus made a U-turn, and Greta switched the side of the bus she was on to wave at Ilse.

Ilse made a heart with her hands, and the bus zoomed off into the distance.

For Leon

June 1940, Maria Alm, Austria

Ilse asked herself a lot of questions about life after Greta left. She didn't exactly have any big revelations, but one thing she thought about stuck on her mind.

What made someone likable? Ilse wondered.

Ilse had no idea how she did it, but Greta easily became *the* most likable person she had ever met. She was always so excited about life and enjoying every moment. Life in Maria Alm was at a standstill without her. When they first met, Ilse hadn't expected for them to start talking like they'd known each other their whole lives. Greta was one of the few people who knew Ilse's true identity. Ilse didn't really know how to explain it, but there's just some people that when you see them, you feel safe. That was Greta. Ilse was glad that she learned more about living life from her. But she still missed her a lot.

Starting fresh was a whirlwind. Greta left so fast, the next day at school the classroom felt empty. Georg didn't seem sullen, or even seem different.

The invasion of Maria Alm was the *third* thing that spun in Ilse's head that warm spring morning.

It really was just a day like any other. After the bus left, Ilse took the somber walk back into town. The sky was orange and the birds were singing louder than ever. It was humid, and Ilse could feel sweat patches building around her armpits.

Ilse wandered back into the town center, up the hill and back to the house. It looked different now. She then remembered the day she came to Maria Alm and it seemed to tower over her. That was just the mindset of a conditioned city girl, really.

Ilse went in through the side door, and the lights were still off. The only illumination came through the windowpane in the kitchen. Ilse poured herself a cup of water and looked at Tante Gisela's library.

The left end of the shelves had beautifully bound first-editions, while the right side had newer paperbacks. *What would books look like eighty years from now?* Ilse thought.

Soft steps descended the staircase, and Ilse turned to the right to see a very sullen Tante Gisela.

She looked tired, but Ilse could tell she tried to maintain a kind expression on her face.

"Good morning," Tante Gisela whispered. Her eyes were dark around the ends and they sagged in parts.

"Morning," Ilse replied.

Tante Gisela strung her satchel over her head and began to slip on her shoes. *She was leaving already?* Ilse thought.

"Late night at the inn," she mumbled. "I've got to get back."

Tante Gisela haphazardly brushed her hair with her long fingers.

"Ilse, I heard about the Leitners leaving town," she added. She sat next to Ilse. "I'm sorry about that. I don't want you to feel lonely."

"I will miss her a lot, but I'm still going to write letters to her. I have Leon. And you," Ilse added.

Tante Gisela smiled. smiled. "Come by the inn later," she said. "We can spend some time together while I work."

Tante Gisela left the door swinging.

After Ilse got her backpack, she headed down the hill. Anton was walking by.

"Good morning, Ilse," he said. His eyes sparkled.

Ilse figured she probably looked groggy and messy at the moment, but she didn't care.

"Good morning," Ilse replied. "I look so gross right now, I-"

"No! You look good," Anton said absentmindedly.

They made their way through the town center, just like Greta and Ilse used to do. Anton stopped to point at the decorations on top of each building. He even skimmed his hand through the fountain as they passed it. Just like Greta.

Once they reached the schoolyard, Ilse noticed that everyone seemed uptight and somber. The little kids weren't running around, and the middle-aged girls huddled in a group next to the building. Lottie, Freya and Georg were gesticulating wildly as the young children watched. They clearly had no idea what the older kids were talking about.

Anton and Ilse strode over just in the nick of time to catch some context.

"…she's right," Georg boasted.

"Nazis are the good in this absurdity… We will prevail!" Freya raised her right hand forward in the Nazi salute.

Lottie cackled, copying her.

Ilse's stomach lurched.

Anton's dark eyes were practically unreadable.

"They're delusional," was all he said. It was enough.

The school bells rung, and everyone huddled inside. It was hot and stuffy as the children of Maria Alm dispersed themselves into different classrooms.

The children filed into their usual desks, and everyone started to unpack their schoolbooks. Ilse gazed at Greta's empty spot.

Fraulein Josephine started scribbling on the board. She did for an eternity, until she clapped out of a sudden.

"Students," she said primly. "We are going to begin our next lesson…"

Ilse didn't hear any of what she said after. She talked and talked, and that's when everyone heard the rumbling. Clipped whispers were seeping through the cracks of the door, and fast, furious footsteps clacked against the old wooden floor.

What was that? Ilse wondered.

The whispers ascended into yells. The door slammed open, and it left a dent in the wall it was pushed onto. German accents spilled into the room, and a group of men appeared behind the door.

A quartet of brazen, haughty men dashed into the room.

The men entered, yelling rapidly in German. Fraulein Josephine stumbled backwards, almost losing her balance. She was visibly shaking.

The men varied quite a bit. A short, blond boy stood the front of the group, while the other three were quite older. They all had dark hair and mustaches. Some were English-style, some were mistletoe.

What they had in common?

A blood-red swastika armband embroidered around their arm.

Ilse's blood immediately left her face. It was a wonder that she didn't pass out. She felt her legs twitching, and her arms started to go numb.

The short blond boy stepped forward and unrolled a scroll of paper.

"We have received information that a Jew has been hidden in the town"—he cut off, glancing down his paper—"the town, Maria Alm. We are here to inspect for hidden people."

He stepped back, and his blotchy red face was returning to a normal color.

They were here for Ilse.

Ilse's heart pounded. *Thum, thum, thum,* was all she heard over the clacks of their heels. Ilse's fingers instantly moistened with sweat, and her muscles were buzzing. She dug her nails onto her thighs to keep from screaming. *What about Leon? Would they search Tante Gisela's house?* A volcano of thoughts erupted in her mind.

One of the older officers scanned the room like a hawk, his hands neatly folded behind his back. He walked slowly around the room, careful to let each of us be aware of his every move.

He looked at Lottie and Freya, narrowing his eyes. He clearly didn't seem to think of them as anything more than useless children.

Scanning the room, Ilse felt just as she did on the train one year ago. He was coming for Ilse. He was coming for *her*. There was no escaping it.

Ilse and the older Nazi locked eyes, but she didn't dare to break the contact. He strode past the desk, his hip brushing Georg's shoulder, to which he paid no mind, until he reached Ilse.

The man tossed his head back and started laughing.

"Schröder, look who we've got," he said, leaning down to Ilse's eye level. One of the men with the mustaches walked up behind him. His breath was pungent and smelled strongly of alcohol. His eyes were an empty sea of nothingness. Ilse didn't see a soul.

Schröder, whom Ilse assumed was the man behind him, was definitely much older. Ilse could see the impact of time on his cheeks and around his eyes, and the glasses that bridged his death stare between hers.

"Get up, foolish girl," Schröder demanded.

Ilse stood, her hands folded at her side. *What was he going to do with me?* Ilse thought. She still pushed her nail into her thigh even further to distract herself.

The other man cackled.

"Look at her hair," the man said. He licked his lips, which made Ilse want to throw up. *Why has my hair done me more bad than good?* Ilse wondered.

"I can see that, Heinrich." Schröder leaned in close to Ilse. "I think we've got a Jew," he whispered.

At the word "Jew", a cool shiver went down Ilse's spine. She tried her best not to shudder, but her hands grew clammy and her feet felt slippery.

"Officer, I think you have a mistake. I am a Catholic," Ilse said fiercely.

The officer called Heinrich slammed his hand on the desk. Ilse didn't dare to flinch.

"I see," Heinrich sneered. "You think I'm blind, idiot girl?"

He stepped back and talked in a quieter, clipped tone to Schröder.

"...*Nein, Nein*... look at her hair... and that nose... she looks like a Jew..." were some of the remarks.

Ilse's blood froze as she pondered what to do. her hands were warm and cold at the same time, but sweaty. Everything around her was full of nervousness and sweat. *Did Tante Gisela know about the Nazis in town? Did she know to tell Leon to stay inside? What if Leon went to play outside?* Ilse was panicking behind a calm complexion.

"We're looking for a boy? ... but I don't think... alright..." Ilse heard bits of their whispers. "So, it's a boy... and other information? ... there's only two here and they don't fit the description.... there's a mother as well? ... it's not anyone here... and a father... the child wouldn't be in school... we have to change our search..."

Ilse didn't catch anymore.

Heinrich let out a crude laugh, and Ilse glanced back at him and his cronies.

"We'll do it and take her," Heinrich said.

His eyes fixated on Ilse. "Stupid girl," he started off with. "Recite a prayer. Go on, go do it," he said, wheezing with horrendous cackles, in sync with the group of Nazi men.

The short blond one joined in. "Yeah, go on. Recite one for us, do a line, eh?"

The men looked absolutely ridiculous. Ilse felt somewhat at peace. She would prove them wrong. Ilse inhaled. If that's what they wanted, then she'd have to deliver.

"Hail Mary, Full of Grace, The Lord is with thee. Blessed art thou among women, and blessed is the fruit of thy womb, Jesus."

The fools stopped at once, clearly taken aback by what Ilse said. Heinrich was the first to speak. He looked suspicious, but a lot less arrogant than before.

"Tell us your name, *girl.*"

"My name is Ilse Kofler," Ilse said calmly. Her pulses had calmed down a lot by now.

The last man, who looked similar to Heinrich had a puzzled expression on his face.

"Heinrich, I don't think that's a Jewish name," Schröder whispered.

"Schröder, you nimwit, she could still be Jewish." Heinrich replied.

Heinrich turned to Fraulein Josephine. "Is this information accurate?" he said, the words biting.

Fraulein Josephine nodded frantically, backing up against the chalkboard.

Ilse had only one thing left to do to solidify her safety.

She raised her hand, just as Freya had done minutes ago. "*Heil Hitler!*" Ilse said loudly.

The men looked up at her. Their armbands seemed to pop out more than they had twenty seconds ago.

"I support your work, and the Reich. Long live Hitler!" Ilse chanted. She tried to sound enthusiastic.

And the facade works every time.

Schröder looked impressed. "Why, if you were a German, you could join the League of German Girls!"

Ilse bowed her head apologetically. "I wish."

Heinrich made eye contact with Schröder, and the rest of group. They all seemed to come to some conclusion that Ilse wasn't who they were looking for.

"I see. And might you have any information as to who this 'hidden Jew' might be?" The officer was no kinder, and he returned to his arrogant manner.

Ilse put a finger to her chin in an attempt to look like she was thinking. After a few moments, she opened her mouth to pretend like she had just had an epiphany.

"I saw a family leave the town this morning," Ilse said, her throat dry. "They were taking tons of suitcases and a whole bus. They were moving to Vienna, is what I heard."

The men looked urgently between one another. "We have to trace the public transport heading to Vienna," one of the men said.

"Communicate to headquarters," Heinrich barked at the blond boy. He stumbled out of the room.

The officers, in one straight line, walked out of the room.

"I didn't know you supported Germany," Lottie later said to Ilse. "I thought you were a fool like Greta."

Ilse could do nothing but nod.

Anton and Ilse left the school in silence. They bumbled along the path, dragging their feet against the ground and watching the dust fly up. Ilse was sweating everywhere.

Anton was the first to speak.

"Did you really mean everything you said?" Anton asked. He gave Ilse a suspicious side view, which she could see through her curls.

Ilse sighed. "I think so."

Anton's expression changed to confused. "You *think* so? Did you even know what you were talking about?"

"Well, I didn't want any trouble with the officers. I don't care for politics," Ilse said, shrugging. She didn't want to say the wrong thing, so she kept her true opinion to a minimum.

Anton's expression softened. "So, you didn't mean what you said."

"No, I guess not," Ilse answered.

They turned into the town center and headed towards the bench.

Anton let out a sigh. "Thank goodness," he said.

Ilse squinted at him. "Why thank goodness?" she questioned.

Anton leant back into the bench and put his arms above his head.

"Swear on your life you won't do or say anything."

"I swear on my life."

"Ilse, I'm the Jew they were searching for." His cheeks turned a light shade of crimson.

Ilse's eyes widened, and she shifted back a little.

"Anton, I didn't mean a word of what I said," Ilse said.

Anton shrugged. "I didn't think so. It didn't seem like something you would say," he said softly. "It was Hansel Gruber."

"Who's Hansel Gruber?"

"Hansel Gruber is the most awful man on Strubergasse," Anton said haughtily. "Strubergasse is where I lived. On the river."

Ilse nodded, trying to understand.

"Hansel Gruber is a drunk who lives on the bottom of an apartment complex in the neighborhood," Anton said. "My *goodness*, he does not know how to mind his own business. He called the police on a boy and his mother who lived above him because he thought they were Jewish. Half the street was up and awake when the poor boy had to jump into the Salzach to get away. Nobody knows where he went, either. The mother was taken away."

"Did you know the boy very well?" Ilse asked.

"The boy was younger than me, so I never got to know him very well. Our mothers were friends," Anton said. "Leon was his name."

He talked about him in the past tense. If only he knew.

"That was the first time I realized the danger of being Jewish. I mean, I knew what was going on in the world for sure. But I'd never seen anything like it. I have three Jewish grandparents. I went to a public school. Nobody really knew much about us."

Anton brushed his hand through the water. "I don't even find it serious to tell who I am. It's no different to me, really."

Ilse smiled.

"One day, Hansel was sitting on a flimsy lawn chair just outside the apartment, and he was chugging a beer. I could practically smell his breath, even though my mom and I were like, ten feet away from him. We had just come back from grocery shopping. Hansel did his normal rants and yells as we passed by. He called my mother horrible names, and he called us 'dirty Jews.' My mother figured that, somehow, Hansel Gruber had figured out we had Jewish heritage. We weren't even *anything*. We were no religion." Anton sighed.

"And so, we packed up our things and moved out to the smallest town my father could find. Maria Alm. Hansel must've reported that a Jewish family was hiding in Maria Alm. I'm sure he found out through talk of the town," Anton said. "Thankfully, he's always drunk so he probably gave a wrong description of what I looked like."

"The people you know can either break or save you, don't you think?" Ilse said, thinking about Frau Kofler.

He shrugged. "I suppose."

The pair said their goodbyes and parted ways soon after, him to the bookstore and Ilse to the house.

The world seemed so much bigger now that she had almost lost it twice.

Ilse rapped at the worn wooden door, and she saw slight marks where her hands had brushed it many times before. The concerned face of Tante Gisela appeared at once.

"Ilse, my goodness," Tante Gisela said, pulling her into a hug.

"Tante Gisela, aren't you supposed to be at work?"

"Never mind that," she said. "I came back to check on Leon and wait for you. I saw the cars."

Tante Gisela quickly rushed Ilse in, and she clambered inside. Leon was laying on the couch, playing with the hem of his shorts.

Ilse dropped her backpack on the floor, rushing over to Leon and throwing her arms around him.

"Leon," Ilse sobbed. "I was so worried about you."

Leon looked very confused, but he embraced the moment and hugged Ilse.

"Ilse, whatever are you talking about?" Leon questioned.

Tante Gisela was gazing over them, like a spell had transfixed her. Ilse could see Tante Gisela's eyes watering, and she removed her glasses to wipe them.

Leon squinted. "Tante Gisela, why are you crying?"

Tante Gisela sat on the chair and smoothed out Leon's shirt.

"I've been thinking of you two like my children," she said. "It was so scary thinking I would lose you both."

Leon smiled. "So, Ilse, what's the reason for the worry?"

Ilse glanced at Tante Gisela, who nodded.

"A small band of Nazis came to the school today, looking for a hidden Jew. They were tipped off," Ilse said.

Leon looked solemn. Ilse didn't' think he understood the extent of what happened, but at least he knew.

"That's fine," he said. "At least you are safe, Ilse."

Ilse threw her arms around him. "I'm just glad *you're* safe, Leon."

Ilse wanted to ask him all about his past and about the dark-haired boy on Strubergasse, but she figured she would save it for another time.

Tante Gisela pulled Ilse outside onto the porch. Ilse noticed for the first time that Tante Gisela had rocking chairs, covered in chipped and faded paint that looked over the town. They sat and rocked for some time.

"Ilse," Tante Gisela said.

"Yes?" Ilse knew what was coming.

"I think it's time I told you," Tante Gisela said. "The boy's home has an opening. My contact can take Leon."

"Send Leon to the home." Ilse stared straight ahead, into the mountains.

It was the right thing to do.

"I'll send postage to meet a car at the Swiss border in Lustenau. We can send for a driver with a Jewish underground organization to meet Leon and exchange him. They will come in July. He'll be safe," Tante Gisela said. "He'll be safe. I know it will be hard to lose him but we'll do it—"

Ilse cut her off. "For Leon," Ilse said. Her gaze remained straight. "We'll do it for Leon."

Tante Gisela gave Ilse a small smile, and looked out into the open green. "For Leon."

Switzerland

July 1940, Maria Alm, Austria

The first letter from Greta came the next month. It was written on faded blue paper in ink that smeared across most of the words. The letter itself was put inside of a used envelope, with the old address and addressee crossed out. Greta wrapped it in old twine, and Ilse could tell it had been used before since the ends came unraveled.

From: Helen Leitner
Kriemhildstrasse 83
A-3371 Maria Alm
AUSTRIA
From: Greta Leitner
Ernstbrunner Strasse 47
A-8043 Graz

AUSTRIA

~~To: Saskia Fellner~~
~~Ernstbrunner Strasse 47~~
~~A-8043 Graz~~
~~AUSTRIA~~
To: Ilse Kofler
Wiehtestrasse 104
A-3371 Maria Alm
AUSTRIA

Dearest Ilse,

*Sorry for the envelope. I could only find this and Mother
didn't want to buy a new one. She wrote a letter to her
sister on this, but it came back in the mail unopened
for some reason. That's the postal service for you.
Mother sent another letter out to her, and we ended up
moving in with her. Tante Saskia is tall and crude.
It's so boring here. I can't believe you let me romanticize
living in a city. It's quite clustery here, though there's
this darling cafe two floors down. I can't even go
out and do anything. Mother keeps me inside. This
week, we tried to boil a potato. It didn't go very well,
so we've resorted to doing nothing. She's looking for
work so we can find a place of our own soon.
I haven't spoken to Father at all. How's Georg doing?
I've never cared for seeing my brother until now.*

*I'm not finishing off the term for this year. Mother thinks
it best to stay with her, and she says I shouldn't worry
about school at a time like this. What can I do but agree?
I miss you so much. I want you to come and visit, but
it's so far away, we will have to wait a long time before
meeting. You must tell me about Anton. He has to be quite
close to you since everyone else in the town is a bore. Has
anything exciting happened? I'll hope to see you soon.*

Greta

Ilse wrote out her response right away.

To my Greta,

*I was surprised to get a letter from you so fast.
For some reason I'd expected it to take longer to
receive a letter. The darn postal service, again.
Just last month, we had a lovely impromptu visit
from a group of Nazis. They were searching
for a hidden Jew. Whoever do you think it
could be? I wonder if they found them.
Sorry about the potato. Vienna is quite interesting,
though I can't say much about recent years. In the winter
season, there's ice-skating rinks and larger-than-life
Christmas markets. I'm sure you'll find something.
Georg is doing fine. I haven't seen or spoken to
him in a while. Anton and I are just friends. He's
quite nice as company, but not the same as you.*

Speaking of which, we've got to find a central spot. Between Graz and Maria Alm. We could take a train there, each of us. I don't think Tante Gisela would let me do it, though. All my best to you and your mother.

Ilse

Ilse sealed the letter in a clean, white envelope and dropped it off in the postal box on her way up the hill.

The sky looked gray to Ilse's left, but was a beautiful cerulean color to her right. Clouds drifted behind and around the mountain aimlessly.

Tante Gisela wanted Ilse to talk to Leon. To prepare him. And that was something Ilse wasn't ready for. It's truly terrifying, saying to goodbye to someone who's been a part of you for a long time. Ilse just tried to keep his best interests in mind.

It was surprising how much a person could age in less than a year. Leon used to be small and meek, but now he had gained weight and height. His cheeky little boy face was growing into a mature boy's face. *What would his mother say if she saw him?* Ilse wondered.

Ilse rapped at the door, and Leon answered.

"Afternoon, Ilse," Leon said.

"You have *got* to brush your hair," Ilse said. "Tante Gisela should trim it for you, too." His hair was much longer and unkempt.

"I will, I will,' Leon said, waving her off.

Tante Gisela was already sitting on the couch. "Ilse, we've received details."

It had been a month, after all. It was early July.

Ilse rushed over, sitting on the arm of the chair. *What were the details? Where would Leon be going? What was going to happen?* Ilse wondered.

Tante Gisela unfolded a slip of paper.

"A car will be sent for Leon to Maria Alm. We will meet them at the bus stop, to be sure no one will see us. July 5th, 1940. 12:00am," Tante Gisela said softly.

"Four days?" Ilse asked.

"That's when they'll get here. Leon will be driven to the Swiss border, where he'll arrive when it's still dark. The Rhine River, a very small river, mind you, will separate Leon and my contact at the monastery. Leon will wade across the river, where a car will be waiting for him. It's a quick drive to St. Gallen after that."

Ilse's heart lifted up, in a way. The plan seemed fairly foolproof.

"Leon will be safe." Ilse said.

"Leon will be safe," Tante Gisela replied.

The pair looked to Leon, who was nodding.

"Thank you for all your help, Tante Gisela," Leon said. "I'm confident this is a good place for me. I'm going to miss this."

Ilse looked at him, an incredulous expression on her face. "Leon, how could you miss this? You've been stuck inside this house for half a year."

Leon sighed. "My family, Ilse. You two. I'm moving into a new identity now. I'm Leon, kind Swiss boy. How does that sound?"

Ilse shrugged. "I'll miss Leon, little Austrian boy," she teased.

Leon looked at Ilse, a longing expression in his eyes.

"What?" Ilse asked.

"I'll miss you too," Leon whispered.

The waterworks came right after. Ilse hugged Leon hard, and she was sure her tears dripped onto his face.

"You're my brother, Leon," Ilse said. "Nothing's going to change that."

Leon looked up at Ilse. "And you're my sister."

Tante Gisela smiled.

"Ilse, I just need help with one more thing," Leon said.

"Leon's been wearing old clothes of my son's that sat around in storage. Can you see if you can find anything new for him tucked away in the storage room?"

Ilse nodded. "I'll see what I can find."

Tante Gisela left to go back to the inn. Ilse went up the long, looming staircase. At the end of the hall was the room, untouched in nearly half a year.

Ilse gently turned the knob, hearing its waning creak. A small bit of dust flew into her face, and Ilse coughed it away. It smelled like a combination of must and mildew.

Clearly, Tante Gisela hadn't been back here in a while. The box with Otto's clothes remained the way Ilse left it.

Ilse opened the box labeled "Otto's clothes, Age 6." The jumper and tees were far too small, and Leon wouldn't be able to fit into them.

Ilse scrummaged through the pile.

"Otto's clothes, Age 7." This was the label for three of the boxes.

Ilse noticed two boxes off to the side, away from the myriad of flappy cardboard and worn tape. These were smooth, and they smelled fresh. They were neatly stacked under a coat rack, with some trench coats and blazers hung above it.

Ilse hauled off the top box, which was barely manageable to hold. She traced her finger along the clear tape on top of it. It was unopened.

Thankfully, Ilse didn't have a habit of biting her fingernails, so they were long and sharp. Sharp enough to pierce through the tape.

Ilse sawed through the box, and came across a yellow piece of paper on stack of a striped shirt:

Boy's clothes, ages 10-12. For Otto in the future.

It hit Ilse like a train.

Otto never got to wear them. Ilse couldn't imagine buying all these clothes and having to tuck them away. Seeing them would bring back memories for Tante Gisela, no matter what.

Ilse pulled out the first shirt she saw, flipping it forward and backward. It would be huge on Leon, but it would certainly work. There were tons of winter clothes in the box when she sifted through, including sweaters, vests, plain white collared shirts, and trousers. Switzerland was cold, wasn't it?

Ilse hauled the box down the stairs.

Leon's mouth was agape as soon as he saw the box.

"Ilse, how on earth could you afford this many clothes?" he said. Leon was picking at his nails, and Ilse could tell he had been biting the skin off his lip. *Was he that nervous to leave us?* Ilse wondered.

Ilse smiled. "Tante Gisela's had them for a while. We had them in the attic," Ilse said.

"I will think of you whenever I wear these," Leon said cheerfully,

Ilse hugged him hard. "You better."

Ilse stayed with the pair for the evening, until it was Leon's bedtime. Tante Gisela coaxed him softly, and he eventually tucked himself in.

Tante Gisela and Ilse retired to the porch, watching the sun wind down for the day. Tante Gisela was sipping on lukewarm tea. Ilse could tell, since she touched the mug and it was room temperature.

"Leon will be gone soon," Tante Gisela said softly.

"I know."

"And how will you be prepared for this change?"

"Tante Gisela, I don't think I ever will be."

Tante Gisela turned to Ilse, and raised her eyebrow. Ilse kept her gaze straight ahead.

"You've been just like his sister, but he's excited. He's excited to start a new life, and it's because of you, Ilse. You have to hold onto that," Tante Gisela said.

She wasn't wrong. Ilse was the reason Leon was alive and well, but Ilse wasn't just a provider for him. She loved him like a brother. It felt nice to have a new family, without feeling the pangs of betrayal to Ilse's parents.

Ilse then realized she learned to love without guilt because of Leon and Tante Gisela.

Tante Gisela was silent for some more time.

"I'm glad you brought Otto's clothes down again."

This time it was Ilse who gave her the side eye, while she gazed obliviously.

"I know you took some before," Tante Gisela said.

"I know," Ilse said. "I know. It's good to repurpose his things, you know. They would just be in the back of a closet if we didn't use it."

"I agree. Stay with Leon as much as you'd like this week. Prep him with everything he needs, and pack with him. We're his only support, and we need to do everything we can for him."

The next morning, Ilse packed Leon's new clothes into an old rucksack, and stuffed more small items into a worn canvas bag that Leon would have to carry.

The day after that, Ilse read all the books she could find, and for one, final time, Leon read *Madeline* aloud to her.

The next day, Tante Gisela told Leon all about Switzerland, with its beautiful blue lakes and endless mountains all around.

And the last night Leon was here, Ilse took him to see the stars of Maria Alm for one last time.

They stayed up late, crying and laughing and crying and laughing. Tante Gisela gave them special permission to walk up the hill as she prepared to meet Leon's driver. Ilse took Leon's hand in hers once it was pitch black, and they dashed through the town and up the hill. The sky was glittering with stars.

They lay in the field late that night, just before the car was due to arrive.

"Ilse," Leon said.

Ilse turned to him, smiling. "Isn't it beautiful?"

She pointed out the Ursa Minor to Leon.

"See the boxed end? ... and then the line extending upwards? That's it," Ilse said.

He squinted, tilting his head left and right. Eventually, he relaxed.

"Can I see the Ursa Minor in Switzerland?" Leon asked.

"I'm not sure," Ilse replied. "We're very close to Switzerland, you know. I'm sure you could."

Leon nodded. "Every night, I'll look for the Ursa Minor. If you do too, we'll match. We'll be in sync," Leon told Ilse.

"Every night, we'll look for the Ursa Minor." Ilse repeated.

"We will," he said.

Soon, they rushed down the hill. Leon hoisted on his pack and looped the tote around his arms. The pair skipped through the town, all the way to the end of the gravel road.

"Shh," Ilse hissed to Leon. "We can't let anyone see us."

Leon giggled, running past the restaurant and circling the fountain before hurrying through the alleyway. A streetlamp clicked on as they ran past.

Ilse could see a light blinking from behind the curve of the hill.

A beautiful lady was leaned against the car. She was dressed professionally, and wore a cap similar to one Ilse had seen Tante Gisela wear around town. Tante Gisela, with her hands behind her back, was talking to her.

Leon and Ilse approached slowly, and the woman took notice of them.

Tante Gisela put her arm around Leon.

"This is Leon," she said.

The woman smiled. "I promise I will take good care of Leon," she said. "You will enjoy your new home."

Leon giggled softly, and eventually the woman's arm was around him.

Ilse hugged Leon hard, and when they parted she could see tears in his eyes.

"Goodbye, sister," Leon said.

"Goodbye, brother," Ilse whispered.

Leon climbed into the car, and Ilse saw his face pressed against the window. Ilse blew him kisses and laughs to mask her anguish. The car powered on, and made a loop at the end of the road, circling back around.

The last thing Ilse saw was Leon's little face. The car left a cloud of dust as it pulled away into the distance and became a tiny dot.

Ilse basked in the smell of the wildflowers and the warm summer air, as she felt Tante Gisela's firm hand pat her shoulder. Ilse felt the pang of loss. Yet she also felt a sense of peace and joy.

That feeling never left her.

21

When All the World is Sleeping

May 1945, Maria Alm, Austria

The war ended five long years later. The sky was blue and bright, and the deep shadow of the maple tree covered the spot where the barn used to stand. Ilse could hear the chirps of the grasshoppers in the warm May air like never before. The clouds, passing through the gaps in the mountains formed distinct shapes. The pine trees seemed to grow taller when Ilse heard the news, and they spread to cover half of the valley. Ilse was nineteen years old.

Leon was living in Switzerland. He left the boy's home last year, based on what Ilse could infer. Nor Tante Gisela or Ilse had spoken to him or had any contact with him. One month after Leon left, they received a note in the mail with two words: *"He's safe."* Tante Gisela and Ilse had received another letter in the mail one year ago with no return postage on it:

To: My sister and aunt
The Inn (no exact address, apologies)
Maria Alm, AUSTRIA

All's well in St. Gallen. Moved in with a darling family in town. I never stopped missing you two.

Much love,
L

Greta was doing well. Ilse and her exchanged cryptic letters over the years, but they didn't meet like they'd dreamt of many times before. Georg moved somewhere far, far away when he turned eighteen, but Ilse never asked where.

That day the war ended, Ilse took an evening walk through the town square, and she planned to head up the path to where the school was. She was sitting on the little bench, dragging her fingers through the water in the fountain. That was when Ilse saw Greta.

Ilse yelled out upon seeing her, thinking she had gone mad. When Ilse turned around, and locked eyes with Greta, she ran and threw herself into Greta's arms. They reconnected like no time had passed, and for that Ilse was so grateful.

Greta wanted to stay, but she had to return home. Universities around the country were opening back up. She was going to enroll in university in Salzburg, and move from Graz. Ilse was home for her last summer break before school. She had enrolled for astrology in Salzburg just after she turned nineteen.

Tante Gisela ran the inn more successfully than ever, and she remained happy in Maria Alm. After Greta left, Ilse met her for dinner at the inn.

Tante Gisela spent the night of the war's end working. The cafe was filled and busy, with people celebrating. "Would I come?" Tante Gisela had asked Ilse. Ilse said she'd drop by later on that night.

Late that night, when all the world was sleeping, Ilse trekked up the hill, dragging her bare feet through the grass. She wore a plaid, blue cotton dress of Tante Gisela's. A mix of pine and lilac filled the air. The sky was clear, and the stars sparkled brighter than ever. Ilse lay in the grass, its soft arms curving around her.

The barn wasn't there anymore, and a big tree loomed over the spot it used to be. A group of farmers came in, took the farming equipment, and knocked Leon's bastion down.

Father would've wanted Ilse to do this. He would've been proud for her to be an astronomer, and to live in the stars like they'd always dreamed. It felt a bit funny to Ilse, but Ilse figured it was because she did it without him. Ilse still looked through the mail every now and then, in the back of her mind thinking she'd receive a letter from them. Or when she spotted someone with red, sleek hair, she felt the urge to reach out and want to loop her arm around theirs. When you love somebody, you never want to give up on finding them.

This is honestly why Ilse had grown to love life. She loved to ponder, and look back on all the decisions she made and how it's gotten her to where she was. *What if I hadn't gone to the coffeehouse that day? What if I hadn't snuck onto the train to Maria Alm? What if I hadn't run up the hill that night and found Leon? What would I have lost?* These questions didn't stop.

"The universe has a way of getting you where you need to be at the right time," Ilse whispered into the clear night sky. Ilse traced the Ursa Minor with her finger. *Was Leon looking at it now? Celebrating the end of it all?* Ilse wondered. She hoped he was.

Everything had worked out.

Who would've thought this is how my life would go? Ilse thought.

She was supposed to be a girl who stayed in the city, who lived with her mother and father, who loved to read and study the sky.

Some parts stuck, didn't they?

Ilse heard the last words Mother and Father uttered to her, the patter of their footsteps sinking into the distance. But Ilse didn't see their sad faces that she last saw. Ilse saw the joyous childhood every child dreamt of. She felt Father and Mother close to her, both lying next to her and high above.

Ilse's parents were dead. After *Kristallnacht,* they were deported to Dachau, where they endured four cruel years of labor. The Germans later moved them to Minsk, Belarus, where they were shot upon arrival.

Tante Gisela had approached Ilse solemnly, while she lay in her bed reading. Frau Kofler had traced her parent's route, she had said to Ilse quietly.

Hope stirred in Ilse briefly, before she saw Tante Gisela's face. Her fingers were cold to the touch as she gently soothed Ilse, while she lay howling and sobbing into her arms. Tante Gisela told Ilse the day before the war ended.

Ilse wondered a lot about where her parents were. *Were they looking at me right now?* Ilse wondered.

"I don't know if you'll come back to me, in memory or in spirit," Ilse whispered into the night sky. "Wherever you are, and however long it takes for you to find me, I promise I'll be here waiting."

Ilse looked up into the sky once more. *Up at the stars we never saw together, Father,* Ilse thought.

"The sadness doesn't ever go away, but it does get smaller over time," Ilse said out loud. "There will always a part of me that will remember your laugh, Father. And your voice too, Mother. And I'll never forget who I lost along the way."

But not everything was lost for good.

The next morning, Ilse took a walk to the entrance of Maria Alm to look at the hills that kept her safe during the war. Ilse sat at the rickety bus stop and stared into the mountains.

A light blue Citroën came tumbling down the road, clouds of dust rising beneath it. Ilse squinted her eyes. Who could possibly be coming to Maria Alm now?

The car stopped a few feet ahead of Ilse, and a middle-aged woman stepped out. Her sunhat covered her hair, but nothing could cover her knowing eyes and well-stitched dress. Her glasses were perched on the end of her nose, just like they had always been.

She came closer, slowly approaching Ilse like she couldn't believe who it was. And then she stopped.

"Well, don't you look grown-up now?"

Acknowledgements

This book would have been impossible to complete without the support, encouragement, and help of many people, a few of whom I would like to thank here.

Thank you to my parents, Jeslyn and Robert Garrabrant, who have always encouraged and supported me in pursuing my passions to the fullest. This book never would have started without my parents, who instilled in me a lifelong passion of reading and writing. Without the endless trips across Europe we have embarked on together, I never would have been inspired to write this novel. I am proud to be their child.

Thank you to my second-grade teacher Mrs. B, who taught me that "a person who can read can write, and a person who can write can read."

Thank you to my developmental editor Claire Evans, who helped to transform my writing into something I never could have attained on my own. Thank you to my cover artist Luisa Galstyan, who created the most beautiful capture of my story to share with the world. Thank you to my formatting designer Charlyn, who worked tirelessly to create a timeless interior.

And most of all, thank you to *you*, reader, for choosing to pick up this book and give it a chance.

ABOUT THE AUTHOR

Emilie Garrabrant is a fifteen-year-old author from Maryland, USA. In her free time, she enjoys traveling, rewatching *Gilmore Girls*, and writing by the fireplace.